W9-DGO-989

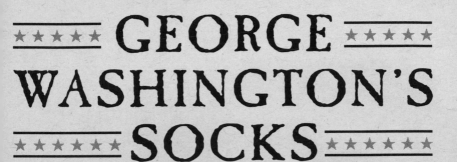

GEORGE WASHINGTON'S SOCKS

SOCKS

A Time Travel Adventure

Special thanks to Jack Stillwaggon of the Revolutionary War Reenactment Group, Mott's Artillery of Randolph, New Jersey, for his historical fact-checking of the manuscript.

This book was originally published in hardcover by Scholastic Press in 1991.

ISBN 978-0-590-44036-3

24 23 22 21 20 19 18 17 16 15 14   14 15/0

Printed in the U.S.A.   40

This edition first printing, September 2010

for
my two adventurous nephews
Matt and Q

with special thanks to
Carol, Nancy, and Mary,
who offered inspiration
one rainy night in the Easton Book Shop!

Other Exciting Adventure Stories
by Elvira Woodruff:

George Washington's Spy
(sequel to *George Washington's Socks*)

Fearless

The Ravenmaster's Secret

The Orphan of Ellis Island

The Magnificent Mummy Maker

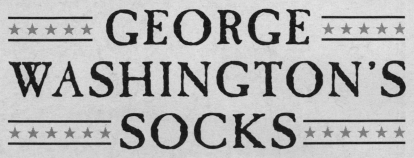

GEORGE WASHINGTON'S SOCKS

A Time Travel Adventure

ELVIRA WOODRUFF

SCHOLASTIC INC.
New York Toronto London Auckland
Sydney Mexico City New Delhi Hong Kong

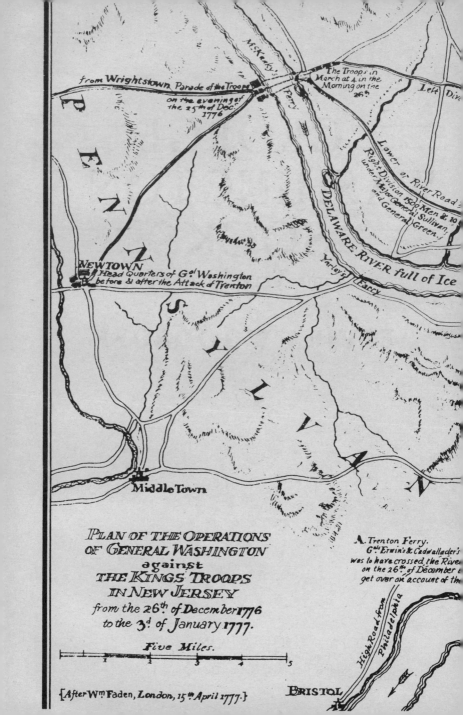

from Wrightstown Parade of the Troops
on the evening of
the 25th of Dec.
1776

McKonky's Ferry

The Troops in
March at 4 in the
Morning on the 26th

Left Div.

PENN

Lower or River Road,
Right Division 1500 Men & 10
under Major General Sullivan,
and General Green.

DELAWARE RIVER full of Ice

NEWTOWN
Head Quarters of Genl Washington
before & after the Attack of Trenton

Yarley's Ferry

SYLVAN

Middle Town

PLAN OF THE OPERATIONS
OF GENERAL WASHINGTON
against
THE KINGS TROOPS
IN NEW JERSEY
from the 26th of December 1776
to the 3d of January 1777.

Five Miles.

| 1 | 2 | 3 | 4 | 5 |

A. Trenton Ferry.
Genl Erwin & Cadwallader's
was to have crossed the River
on the 26th of December but
get over on account of the

High Road from Philadelphia

BRISTOL

{After Wm. Faden, London, 15th April 1777.}

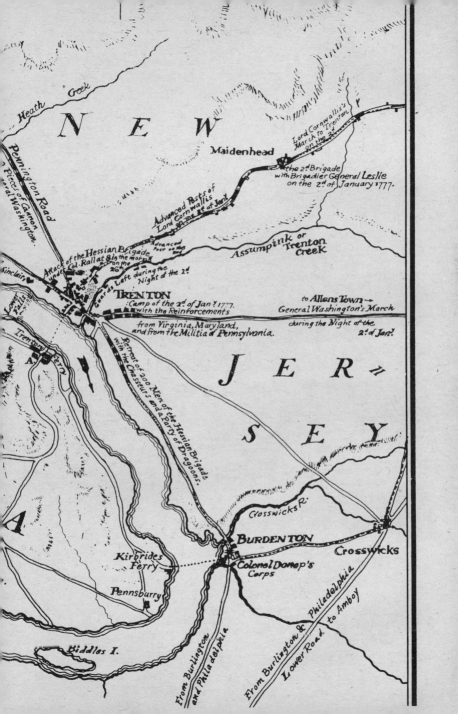

One

MATTHEW CARLTON, you're not leaving this table until you've finished those peas," Mrs. Carlton said firmly.

"But, Mom, I've got to finish packing," Matt pleaded. "It's our first official club camp-out tonight, and since I'm president of the club I've got to make sure that we have everything we need."

"What's this about a club and a camp-out?" Mr. Carlton asked, putting a forkful of noodles in his mouth.

"Matt and some of the boys in the neighborhood have started a club and they want to sleep out tonight," Mrs. Carlton told him.

"It's not just a goofy club, Dad, like stamp collectors or something. It's an adventure club. Tony, Hooter, Q, and I are all members. We meet and talk about real adventures that people have had throughout history. Q gave the club this old set of books that his uncle had given him called *Great Adventures in History*. At every meeting we're going to read about one adventure. The first one that we picked out is the crossing of the Delaware by George Washington and his army during the Revolutionary War. Q and I did our history report on George Washington, so we know a lot of stuff already that we can tell the other members. We're going to camp out tonight in Tony's yard. It was my idea to start the club in the first place, so I'm the president. I've got a lot of things to check on, so can I please be excused?" Matt began to stand up.

"Hold on, champ," his father chuckled. "You're club sounds fine but you've got peas on your plate that your mother wants you to finish. Just think of them as an adventure in eating. Go on now and finish them up."

Matt groaned. "I'd rather face a bloodthirsty vampire, or a wild cat, or a . . ." Soon he was lost in thought while imagining all the things he'd rather face than the pile of disgusting green things on his plate. The phone suddenly rang in the kitchen, bringing him back to the reality of the dinner table. He watched as Mr. Carlton got up to answer it. Then Matt stole a glance at his little sister, Katie, who was sitting across from him, playing with the noodles on her plate. With one hand she poked her fork in and out of the noodles and with her other hand she twisted one of her bright red curls around her finger.

2

"Katie Carlton, how many times do I have to tell you to stop twisting that hair?" Mrs. Carlton sighed as she got up and went to the refrigerator.

Timing, Matt was thinking. *It's all a matter of timing*. Quickly he reached over and took the lid off the sugar bowl, then dropped in all the peas from his dish. He placed the lid back on a second before his mother returned to the table. Then he glanced back at Katie, whose mouth had dropped open as she stared at the sugar bowl.

"Oh, great," Matt moaned to himself, giving her a hard cold stare, but Katie had begun to giggle. Mr. Carlton got off the phone and returned to the table. He picked up his glass of iced tea.

"Honey, did you want more sugar for that?" Mrs. Carlton asked, passing the sugar bowl to her husband. Mr. Carlton took the sugar bowl and placed it beside his plate. "Um, no, I think I'm fine," he said.

Katie was unable to suppress herself, and before too long was doubled over in her seat, giggling. "And just what is all that about, Katherine?" Mrs. Carlton asked, looking over to Katie.

"Nothing, Mom," Matt reassured her. "You know how silly she gets when she starts to play with her food. She was just making the noodles wiggle on her plate like worms. Weren't you, Katie?" Matt pinched her arm from under the table. "*Ow!*" Katie said, lifting her arm and pointing to the sugar bowl.

"How would you like to come camping with our

club tonight, Katie?" Matt blurted out. He was desperate. He couldn't risk his parents handing out any punishments tonight. He could just imagine having to explain to the guys that their president couldn't make the first adventure of their club because his parents were punishing him for filling the sugar bowl with peas!

Katie quickly put down her arm and beamed with delight. "Oh, boy, I'm going camping with Matt!"

"That's good of you to include your sister." Mr. Carlton smiled at Matt.

"Yes, it's very nice of you." Mrs. Carlton smiled. In fact everyone was smiling, everyone except Matt.

Great, he thought to himself. *My first adventure with the club and I have to drag along a girl! A seven-year-old baby girl!* He glared at Katie, who grinned back, giving one of her curls a twist.

Two

AN WE GO HOME and get my blanket?" Katie's voice came from inside the tent. The first meeting of the Adventure Club had just come to order. President Matthew Carlton had taken attendance, collected dues (twenty-five cents or equal amounts of candy), and had ordered Katie to wait in the tent.

Matt shook his head in disgust as he sat at the campfire with the other club members, Tony, Q, and Hooter.

"Go to sleep, Katie. We can't get your blanket now. It's too late," he called over the crackling of the campfire. Q handed Matt a thick green book. The words ADVENTURES IN HISTORY: VOLUME FOUR were printed in large gold letters on the cover. Matt looked over to Tony and Hooter.

"Q and I did our history report together on George Washington," he told them. "So if you have any questions, we can probably answer them, since we did so much research."

"You only read one library book for that report," Tony objected. "You can't call one book 'so much research.' "

"You didn't see the size of that book, Tony," Matt told him. "It was big. I mean really big."

"Look, Tony, we're not saying that we know everything about the Revolutionary War, but we did do a report on it and we do know more than you do," Q said smugly.

"Okay, guys, let's not waste any more time trying to decide who knows more about the Revolutionary War. Q got this book from his uncle and none of us have read it yet. So be quiet and listen." Matt opened the book to the page that had a bookmark in it.

" 'The Crossing of the Delaware River and the War for Independence,' " he began. " 'Between the autumn of 1775 and the autumn of 1776, the rebel army had suffered such great losses that many feared the American cause was soon to be lost.' "

"I thought we won the war," Hooter interrupted. "It sounds like we lost it."

"We almost did lose it," Matt told him, looking up from the book. "That's why this adventure is so incredible. Listen." Matt looked back down to the book and continued to read.

" 'As he made his way across New Jersey, General Washington was in desperate need of food and supplies for his ill-clad army. New Jersey was at this time a state divided in its loyalties. Many farmers felt that they still owed their allegiance to King George, and would not accept the new confederate money that the Congress had issued to the army. British spies were everywhere. The rebels themselves were ill-trained and inexperienced soldiers, most of them having more experience with a plow than the bayonet. If these were not enough obstacles for General Washington, the winter of 1776 proved to be the harshest weather that the region had ever experienced.

" 'But, as discouraged as Washington was, he was not prepared to accept defeat, not yet. The American Army was on the verge of collapse, and in desperate need of a victory in order to turn the tide in their favor. The crossing of the Delaware and the taking of Trenton on December twenty-sixth proved to be just such a victory.' Can you imagine what it must have been like?" Matt said suddenly, looking up from the book.

"Cold," Q replied. "Really, really cold. They crossed the river at night, in the middle of rain and ice and snow. They must have been freezing."

"Just like we're going to be if we let this fire go out," Tony said as he got up to get another log for the fire. Matt put down the book and joined the other club members in carrying over a load of wood from the woodpile to the campsite. Tony's dad had helped them to build the fire after they had set up the tent behind the garage. He had given them a long lecture on fire safety before he finally left them alone and went back into the house.

Matt thought camping in Tony's yard was okay, but he wished it were a little more wild and dangerous. If Tony's father had let them make camp along the lake like they had wanted to do, it would have been perfect. As it was, Tony's parents kept coming to the kitchen door and peeking out to check on them every ten minutes.

"Sometimes they treat me like I was in second grade or something," Tony groaned, waving his mother away from the door.

"It's probably because you're so small," Q pointed out.

"Yeah, Tony, you know, I've seen some second-graders that are a whole lot bigger than you," Hooter added. Tony shrugged his shoulders. He was used to people pointing out his height or lack of it. He was the shortest boy in the fifth grade.

"It's just because of his size that Tony is such an important member of the club," Matt said with authority, sitting back down in front of the fire.

"It is?" Tony squeaked, sitting beside him.

"Sure, since you're the smallest man, you'll be our scout. You can do all the tracking, traveling ahead of us to check things out without being seen. And since you're so small you weigh less than any of us. Do you remember those Indian scouts in the Davy Crockett book we read? Remember how they could walk through the woods without making a sound? Well, you don't think they weighed three hundred pounds, do you?"

"No, I guess not." Tony grinned, throwing his shoulders back and sitting up straight like an Indian scout.

Matt turned to Q. Q's name was Quentin but everyone called him Q for short. "Now, Q, you'll be the club's brain," Matt told him. "Everyone here knows that you have the fastest brain in the fifth grade, maybe even the whole school."

"Except for Carla Ponti," Tony interrupted.

"Have you seen what Carla Ponti looks like lately?" Hooter said with a grin. "She had her hair permed or something and it looks like a brillo pad that's been microwaved."

"Not too smart. But then she's a girl. What do you expect?" Matt shook his head. "Now, Q, we're going to need some quick thinking if we get in some live-or-die situations. So be prepared to think."

"I know," Q said, taking off his glasses to wipe a mosquito from them. "I already thought of that and I have no intention of perming my hair."

"So what about me?" Hooter interrupted. "What's my job?" Hooter's real name was Brian Melrose, but he didn't look anything at all like a Brian Melrose. To Matt he had always looked like a young version of Fred Flintstone. He was big and kind of goofy-looking, but he was a softy at heart. In the third grade he had found a baby owl with a broken wing.

He put it in a little box and carried it with him wherever he went, hooting softly to it all the while. His parents finally made him take the owl to the animal shelter, but by then he had done so much hooting that all the kids in the neighborhood had started calling him "Hooter" and the name just stuck.

"Don't worry, Hooter. I've got a big job for you," Matt assured him. "You'll be our strong man. Whenever we find ourselves in a situation that takes abnormal strength and more muscle than we can muster, we'll turn to you. And if we come across any stray baby animals, that will be your department. What do you think? Can you handle it?"

"Piece of cake, Chief." Hooter grinned, flexing his muscles. Then he suddenly stopped and looked toward the tent. Matt and the rest of the boys followed Hooter's gaze. Everyone was quiet, listening to the little voice coming from the tent.

"What's my job, Chief?" Everyone looked at Matt and grinned but Matt frowned instead.

"Forget it, Katie." He scowled. "No girls are allowed in the Adventure Club," he said firmly. The little voice answered.

"I'm not a girl. I'm a sister."

"No, Katie, what you are is a pain. Now be quiet and go to sleep." The only reply from the tent was some loud sniffling.

"Oh, Matt, have a heart." Hooter stood up and

walked toward the tent. "Why can't we make her a visiting member, just for tonight?"

"Technically speaking, the club's charter dictates that no females are allowed in the club, visiting or otherwise," Q told him.

"Okay, okay. But it's like Katie said, she's not just a girl. She's a relative. That should count for something," Hooter pointed out.

"None of you guys have a little sister, and believe me you don't know what pains they can be," Matt tried to explain.

"I sort of know how she feels," Tony said. "It's not much fun always being the littlest and the one that always gets left out."

"Come on, Matt, just for tonight. She can't be that bad." Hooter laughed, opening the tent.

"Okay." Matt sighed. "But don't say I didn't warn you." As Hooter held open the tent flap, the newest temporary member of the Adventure Club stumbled out. In the light of the campfire her head was a blaze of red curls. Over her shoulder was a toy bow, with the arrows in a pouch on her back. She held a water gun in one hand and a plastic Heroic Hero sword in the other. She took a step toward the group and shot Hooter in the nose with her squirt gun.

"I'm ready for the adventure, Chief," she said with a dimpled grin.

Three

"HEN DO WE GO on the adventure?" Katie asked impatiently.

"Well, this is . . . this is it," Matt said, feeling a little embarrassed.

"Oh," Katie replied with a disappointed look. Suddenly all the club members began to feel as embarrassed as their leader. When they had planned the camp-out it had seemed like it would be a great adventure, but now, looking around at Tony's backyard, with the swing set and the car in the driveway, it didn't seem adventurous at all. Matt's face brightened as he looked past the yard and into the woods.

"You know when we first planned this camp-out we were going to camp along the lake, because it would be like Washington and his men camping alongside the Delaware River," Matt said, thinking out loud.

"That would have been great if our parents hadn't all said no." Q sighed.

"They said no to camping along the lake, but they didn't say no to taking a hike there," Matt pointed out.

"Well, I guess we can try and ask them tomorrow," Tony said as he watched the lights going off in his house.

"I wasn't thinking about tomorrow," Matt whispered.

"You woorn't?" Hooter whispered back, his mouth full of marshmallows.

"No, I was thinking about tonight."

"Tonight!" Hooter, Q, and Tony all repeated at once.

"It's going to be kind of hard to ask them tonight." Tony motioned to his darkened house. "Looks like my parents have gone to bed. I think we should wait and get their permission."

"What could be wrong with a little hike?" Matt pleaded. "Besides, it would be great for the club. We don't just want to read about adventures. We want to have them, too. Some of those rebel soldiers were only a few years older than we are. Once they crossed the river they had to walk for nine miles, in the dark, in a snowstorm. And when they reached Trenton they had to fight for their lives. Come on, Tony, compared to that a little walk along a lake is no big deal."

"I don't know," Tony hesitated. "I don't want to get into trouble."

"Technically speaking, we aren't disobeying anyone," Q pointed out. "Since none of our parents said anything about a hike, we don't know whether they would mind or not." Q rubbed his chin just the way he had seen Sherlock Holmes do in a movie. Sherlock Holmes was Q's hero.

"What are they talking about?" Katie whispered as she sat down next to Hooter.

"I'm not sure," Hooter whispered back, handing her the bag of marshmallows. "But I think we're going somewhere."

After a bit more discussion, it was decided that the club would extend their first adventure from the camp-out to a hike. And not just any hike, but a night hike along the lake. To get there all they had to do was follow the path through Tony's woods. They had all been on the path before, but never at night. Tony seemed the most hesitant.

"I don't know if this is such a hot idea," he said.

"Don't worry," Matt tried to assure him. "Your parents have gone to sleep and they'll never have to know about it." He stood up. "We'll leave the fire going for you, Katie. There are still some hot coals burning. You be a good girl and go to sleep in the tent. It's too dangerous for little kids out there." He pointed ominously in the direction of the woods.

"I'm not a little kid," Katie said indignantly. "I

want to go with the club. I want to go with you, Mattie-o."

"Look, Katie, you can have that whole bag of marshmallows all to yourself. You don't have to share them with anybody." Matt tried coaxing her, but Katie wouldn't budge.

"If you don't let me come I'll go and tell Tony's mom to call Mom and Dad. I'm going to tell them that you went on a hike to the lake and you wouldn't take me," she countered. Matt let out a loud sigh. He knew when he was beat.

"Okay, but if you act up, even once, you're out of here. Understand?"

"I don't think this is such a good idea," Q said, shaking his head at Katie, who scowled in his direction. "What if she falls in the lake? Or what if she gets lost? Or what if — "

"What if she tells Tony's parents where we are?" Matt interrupted.

"You have a point there," Q conceded.

"Then it's settled. We're all going so let's put out the fire," Matt said, kicking some dirt over the still glowing coals. Everyone stood up and did the same. Katie grinned and fired her squirt gun at Q.

"Hey!" he yelled, for it was a direct hit on his glasses.

"You'd better save your ammunition, kid," Hooter told her. "We might need it for later on." Everyone began to make jokes about Katie's vast array of weapons and how she would carry the club's arsenal in case of attack. It was easy to laugh and joke in the safety of Tony's yard but as they entered the woods they soon grew quiet.

"It sure is dark in here," Katie whispered.

Four

"I BET THIS PLACE is crawling with snakes," Hooter said, shining his flashlight on an old log alongside the path.

"I don't care as much about snakes as spiders," Q grimaced. "Just the thought of walking into a web gives me the creeps." He adjusted his glasses on his nose, as he always did when he was feeling uneasy.

"Snakes and spiders are nothing to worry about." Tony turned around to tell them. He had tried scouting ahead but only had the courage to go a few feet before the group.

"Tony's right," Matt said, sounding as fearless as he could. "There's nothing to be afraid of."

Suddenly the loud screech of a hawk echoed through the darkness and all the members of the Adventure Club found themselves huddling together in the shadows of the pine trees. Katie shot her water

17

gun in the direction of the hawk and everyone listened as the strange and unfamiliar noises of the night filled the woods. The moonlight filtered through the trees, creating a sea of shadows that seemed to shift and sway in the breeze. The leaves rustled above their heads as they felt a sudden draft on their necks. They could smell the cold dampness of the lake in the air.

Tony was the first to speak. "I didn't say there was nothing to be afraid of," he whispered. "I just meant that spiders and snakes are nothing compared to the legend of the lake. Now, that's really creepy."

Matt gripped Katie's hand tighter. "What legend of the lake?" he asked uneasily. Tony made his way back to the path, moving very slowly and turning around every now and then as he spoke. The rest of the club trailed behind him.

"The last time I went to visit my grandfather in the nursing home he told me about the legend of Lake Levart."

"Wait a minute," Matt interrupted him. "Was he talking about this lake? This is Levy Lake. He must have had his lakes mixed up."

"No," Tony continued. "He was talking about this lake, all right. He said that years and years ago it was called Levart Lake and that over time people began calling it Levy Lake. He was born here a long time ago and he knows all that kind of stuff."

"So what's the big deal?" Hooter asked. "They

18

changed the name of the lake. What's so creepy about that?"

"What's so creepy is that there was something strange going on in the lake, like it was haunted or something," Tony whispered.

"Was there a ghost?" Katie whispered back, her eyes growing big as she brandished her sword toward the shadows.

"Well, no. No one ever saw a ghost, but people would disappear and it wasn't as if they just drowned, because they never found their bodies," Tony continued.

"Did any of them ever come back?" Matt asked with a shiver, for the breeze had suddenly picked up.

"Some of them did," Tony told him. "But they seemed to disappear for a while and when they did come back they were never the same. They all had fantastic stories to tell and they would sit by the lake for hours, just staring, like they were crazy or something. And the really strange thing is that all these people, the ones that never came back and the ones that did, all of them had gone out on the lake in a rowboat."

"What's so strange about that?" Q interrupted. "It is a lake and lots of people go out on boats."

Tony stopped on the path and shook his head. "Grandpa said that none of the people had a boat. He knew because when his best friend, Adam Hibbs, disappeared, my grandpa had been with him.

They'd been a little bit older than us, and had been camping out along the lake. They were sleeping in their tent when Adam got up. He said that he was thirsty and was going to get his canteen that he had hung on a tree. My grandpa heard his footsteps outside the tent and then he heard what sounded like someone getting into a boat. He waited and when Adam didn't return he got up and went out to look for him, and guess where he was?"

"Where?" Hooter whispered.

"He was out on the lake in a rowboat, a rowboat my grandpa had never seen before. Grandpa said that it was a three-quarter moon and in all the light he could see Adam's face as he rowed to the middle of the lake. And he was smiling, smiling like he'd never smiled before. My grandpa tried calling to him, but either he didn't hear him or he wouldn't listen, because he never looked back to the shore." Tony stopped to take a breath. Suddenly a raccoon screeched in the darkness and everyone automatically drew closer together.

"Then what happened?" Matt asked, trying to keep the nervousness out of his voice.

"A cloud must have drifted across the moon because it suddenly got dark and Grandpa ran to the tent to get a lantern. But when he got back to the lake it was too late. Adam Hibbs was gone, disappeared, boat and all, and no one to this day knows what happened to him. There were five more cases of people disappearing over the next fifty years, and

Grandpa investigated all of them. He could never put to rest what had happened to his friend, and so when these other people disappeared, he was right there asking questions and looking for clues. The only thing that my grandfather ever uncovered was that there was always this rowboat, and the disappearances always happened under the same moon." Tony was speaking now in a hushed whisper. "It was always a three-quarter moon."

Five

MATT FELT THAT as the leader of the club he had to be the bravest but the more he heard about this lake business the less brave he became. It took all his courage to begin to walk down the path toward the lake.

"Come on, guys. We're almost there," he said. Tony took his place in the scout's position and the group reluctantly followed.

"Levart Lake, that's a strange name for a lake. Do you think it was named after someone named Levart?" Q wondered aloud, trailing after Matt and Katie.

Tony turned around to answer. "Grandpa was just beginning to tell me what he had figured out about that name. He said it was a clue to the mystery and he felt sure he was on to something. But then my mother came back into the room. She was in the kitchen talking to the dietician about Grandpa's meals. He's got this thing about eating yellow. He won't eat anything yellow. Anyway, as soon as my mom came back he stopped talking and winked at me. He's funny that way, likes to keep secrets."

"Did you ever think that he might be a little batty?" Hooter called from the back of the line, for they were now all walking single file. "You know how some old people get," he continued. "They spend so much time just sitting around that they stop eating stuff that's yellow and start making up stories."

Tony's face flushed red as he turned around to face Hooter. "Maybe your grandfather is batty and makes up stories but mine isn't," he said emphatically.

"Whose grandfather are you calling batty?" Hooter came up to the front of the line and towered over Tony.

"Look, you two," Matt interrupted. "No one is calling anyone's grandfather batty. We're all in this club together and we can't be fighting with each other. We have to depend on one another like the rebels did. We're comrades, remember? So cut it out and shake," he ordered. Hooter reluctantly put out his hand and he and Tony shook, trying not to look at each other in the process.

"Agh!" Q suddenly let out a scream. "I knew it! I knew I was going to walk into a web!" he moaned as he tried to get a sticky spiderweb off of his face. Katie was able to help him get untangled with her sword. She even offered to wash his glasses with

23

her squirt gun. Meanwhile Tony had regained some of his bravery and was scouting ahead.

"We're almost to the lake," he called back to them. "It's just down this bank. Once we're off the path and out of the woods, we'll be able to see better. The moon is almost full."

"Yeah, what phase would you say the moon is in tonight?" Matt asked, looking up.

Suddenly they all stopped and were looking up at the bright orb that hung above the trees.

"Three-quarter," Q said with authority. He had read all the astronomy books in the school library. "Definitely a three-quarter moon."

"Are you thinking what I'm thinking?" Matt asked uneasily.

"That's just what I was thinking. In fact I was already thinking it five minutes ago," Q said, adjusting his glasses on his nose.

"Aw, come on, you guys," Hooter said. "You don't believe that old story about the moon and some boat, do you? And I'm not saying that your grandfather is batty or anything, Tony. Maybe he just had a great imagination."

"My marshmallows," Katie murmured. "I dropped my marshmallows." But Matt and the rest of the club were so busy discussing the legend again that no one paid any attention to Katie. In fact it was almost another ten minutes before anyone noticed she was missing.

When he finally realized that Katie was no longer beside him, Matt began calling her name and shining his flashlight into the shadows. "I should never have let go of her hand." He sighed. "Katie, Katie. Can you hear me Katie?"

"It's all my fault." Q shook his head as he pointed his flashlight up and down the path. "She put down the bag of marshmallows to help me when I got caught in that spiderweb."

"No," Matt insisted. "It's my fault. I'm the president of the club and I should never have let her come. If anything happens to her I — "

But he never finished his sentence for there was suddenly a loud splash followed by the sound of rippling water. Matt immediately turned toward the direction of the splash and everyone followed him down the path, running as fast as they could.

Once out of the woods, they found themselves standing on a small incline just above the shore. The lake stretched out before them, lit in the eerie white glow of the moonlight. And floating on the silvery ripples of its surface was a boat. An empty old rowboat! Matt and the rest of the boys stood transfixed, watching as the breeze picked up and gently sent the lonely craft on its course to shore.

"Oh, no!" Matt gasped, his eyes following the boat to the lake's edge. For there on the pebbled beach stood a little figure with red curls blowing back on her head as the early autumn breeze swept across the water. She stood perfectly still, as if waiting for the boat, and when it finally reached her, she smiled a very strange smile.

"Katie, no!" Matt cried out, but it was no use. His little sister was climbing into the boat. Her legs were so short that she was having a hard time hoisting herself over the side.

"Katie, stop! Get away from it," Matt yelled frantically, but still Katie paid no attention.

When he first laid eyes on the empty boat floating in the moonlight, Matt was filled with a sense of wonder mixed with fear.The very emptiness of the boat seemed to be beckoning to him to come and fill it. None of the boys could speak at first; they were overcome with a strange longing to board the lonely craft. Standing on the incline, still at a distance from the boat, Matt also felt a terror rising within him. There was something very wrong with this vessel, something dangerous and powerful. A strange force seemed to be present.

Matt knew, deep down, that they should run from this thing, run as far away as they could. But the sight of his sister caught in this mysterious force sent him running straight for it, instead.

Hooter, Tony, and Q had the same mixed feelings, but when Matt took off to rescue Katie, they didn't hesitate to join him. They were all yelling at Katie to get away from the boat when they suddenly came to within a few feet of it. Matt was just ahead of them, and so he was the first to come under the boat's spell. It was the same desire to board the boat that he'd felt when he first saw it, only now the desire had become overwhelming.

All of his fear and mistrust were suddenly gone. The tautness left his face. The lines on his forehead disappeared as Matt began to smile! He reached out for Katie and lifted her into the boat. Then he climbed in himself.

Q and Tony did the same. Hooter gave the boat a shove and jumped in after them. Smiling, as if in a trance, Matt reached for an oar. Q reached for the other one and they began rowing toward the center of the lake, the smiles never leaving their faces.

When a large cloud drifted across the moon, the old rowboat and its smiling crew were suddenly engulfed in a thick velvety darkness. An iridescent mist began to slowly swirl about them as they sat motionless. Q and Matt were on one seat, and Tony and Hooter on the other, with Katie kneeling on the floor between them. A low whistling sound seemed to circle them as the boat began to tremble, and the mist wrapped around them like a cocoon.

When the three-quarter moon finally returned from behind a cloud, the lake stretched out smooth as glass beneath it. The old rowboat and her adventurous crew were gone! Vanished! It was as if the lake had swallowed them up. The only evidence that remained of the mysterious craft and her spellbound sailors were the silvery ripples that fanned out from the lake's center. As the wind picked up, it blew across the sparkling surface, smoothing out the uneven choppiness of their departure. All that remained was the gentlest hint of a wave.

Six

BEFORE MATT EVEN OPENED his eyes, he knew that something was wrong. The quiet stillness of the lake had suddenly been replaced by the loud roar of a river at flood stage! As he sat blinking in the darkness, Matt could hear the chattering of his teeth and feel the tips of his ears stung with the cold.

Cold? he thought to himself. *Why is it so cold all of a sudden?* When he was finally able to focus his eyes, he saw Tony and Hooter sitting across from him, with Katie on the floor at their left. He turned to see Q sitting beside him in the boat.

"Boat!" Matt cried. "We're in the boat! How . . . how did we get here? And it's snowing! How can it be snowing in September?" But his question went unanswered as the roar of the river drowned out his feeble cry. He and the rest of the horrified crew clung to the sides of the boat as it rushed down the swollen river. The little craft dipped and dived, dangerouly crashing into large chunks of ice.

Matt wondered if he could help to steady their course with his oar but he was too terrified to let go of his hold on the side of the boat. Everyone, down to the last man, was holding on for dear life. The only lady on board, however, had other ideas. Matt looked on in horror as Katie tried to stand up in the middle of the boat!

The current was so strong and the river so deep and choked with ice, that Matt knew if his sister were to fall overboard, she would probably never survive. Hooter must have been thinking the same thing for at the exact moment that Matt lunged forward to reach for Katie, Hooter did the same.

With the sudden shift in weight, the old rowboat veered sharply to the right. Hooter and Matt fell over together onto Tony. Everyone was yelling, trying to untangle themselves. It wasn't until they'd finally sat up and looked at the empty space in the middle of the boat, that they were all stunned into a deathly silence. Matt was the first to break it.

"Katie! Katie!" he screamed, wild-eyed into the night. "Where are you?" But the only reply was the roar of the river and the crash of the ice. Their boat had come to an abrupt stop, as it sat lodged between two thick ice floes. The snow that had been falling was mixed with freezing rain, but Matt took no notice.

"Please, Katie, answer me. Where are you?" he cried, leaning over the side of the boat. They all took turns calling her name and waiting for an answer, but none came. They sat for a long time, dazed, unable to believe what had happened. Meanwhile the freezing rain lashed their faces and soaked through their sweatshirts. Q was the first to notice it.

"We've got to get out of this ice jam or we'll freeze to death," he called to Matt, but Matt was too distracted to hear. He was desperate to see some sign of Katie. He knew that if he could just see her, he'd jump out of the boat and save her. He wanted to jump out now, but the visibility was so bad there was no telling where she was. He felt as if a sea of blackness had swallowed her up and the thought of his little sister struggling under the icy water was more than he could bear. He sat unable to move, paralyzed with fear and grief, watching the tiny beam of Q's flashlight in the darkness. His eyes were filled with tears as he buried his head in his hands. He thought of his mother, and how he would have to tell her what had happened to Katie. He thought of his father and he could see the look of disbelief and pain in his father's eyes.

"Katie, please don't be dead. Please, Kate," he sobbed, and once he began crying he couldn't stop. Hooter traded seats with Q and put his arm around Matt.

"It's all my fault, Hoot. It's all my fault," Matt cried.

"Come on, Matt, it wasn't your fault. It was an accident." Hooter tried to console him.

Meanwhile, as Q moved over to Hooter's seat, his flashlight shone on the inside of the boat. In the glow of the flashlight he and Tony both noticed the cracked white letters next to Hooter's seat. Q held the light over the inscription, as Tony read it aloud.

" 'Emit Levart.' " They looked at each other and then back at the inscription. "Levart Lake," Tony whispered. "That's what my grandfather was telling me, about the lake being called Levart Lake. He said the mystery of the lake was somehow tied up in the name Emit Levart." But the wind had picked up and Tony's words were lost in a gale of freezing rain as he traced his frozen fingers over the chipped letters.

Seven

SUDDENLY A LOUD CRASHING of ice could be heard, along with the muffled voices of men. When Q turned the flashlight in their direction the sight that met his eyes could not have been more welcome.

"Matt! Look! It's Katie! It's Katie! She's on that ice over there! And look, she's alive!" he yelled.

"Matt! Help me!" Katie cried. "I'm over here."

As Matt wiped the tears from his eyes and looked toward the beam of light, he was overcome with relief, for he could just make out the figure of his little sister, and could barely hear her cries that were lost in the roar of the river. She was stumbling about on an ice floe that had come to rest alongside a large wooden boat. At that moment the flashlight batteries gave out and all was darkness again.

"She must have landed on the ice when she fell out of the boat!" Matt exclaimed. "She's alive! She's alive!" He was laughing and crying at the same time as Hooter and the others whooped for joy.

"And there's another boat!" Q cried. "We can all be rescued."

"Help! Help!" Tony and Hooter cried out in unison. They could hear voices getting closer.

"We're coming, Katie," Matt yelled as loudly as he could. But their cries were met with a sudden silence.

Then out of the darkness a deep voice commanded, "Halt, in the name of the Continental Army!"

"Halt?" Tony whispered. "Is he kidding?"

"The Continental Army? Did he say the Continental Army?" Q asked, wiping the sleet off his glasses. Everyone in the boat was peering in the direction of the voice, when Matt suddenly sat back in his seat. He had just gotten a glimpse of the long wooden boat as it nudged its way between the ice floes.

Huddled in the craft were a group of men in tattered clothes. Some were wearing tricornered hats, and others had rags wrapped around their heads. Their faces were raw and weathered, and they were each clutching long guns in their rag-covered fingers.

Matt breathed a sigh of relief as he watched a tall man in a dark cape reach over the boat's side and pull Katie from the ice floe. He quickly wrapped her in his thick cape and handed her to one of the men

34

beside him. Matt was so overcome with relief that he was unable to talk, even though he had wanted to call to Katie and let her know that he was there.

As he stood staring from the old rowboat, Matt couldn't take his eyes off the man who had rescued her. He was a tall imposing figure in a blue and buff uniform. Matt had the strange feeling that he knew the man, for his figure was unmistakable, with his white hair rolled on the sides, and tied in the back with a ribbon. His face was strong and proud. It was the face of a leader, the face of a determined man. His eyes stared straight into Matt's, as if one commander had recognized another. It took all of Matt's courage to speak.

"My . . . sister. Is she all right?"

"The child is alive. No harm will come to her."

"Who . . . who are you?" Matt stammered.

"General George Washington, Leader of the Continental Troops," came the firm reply.

"This is some kind of joke, right?" Matt mumbled. The general was not smiling, however, as the wind lashed the freezing rain and snow all about them.

"You had better explain what business brings you out on the river this night and whether you be friend or foe to the Revolution," the general called above the roar of the river.

He doesn't seem like a crazy man, Matt thought as he observed the fierce determination on the general's face. Matt looked at the faces of the other soldiers in the boat. They didn't seem crazy either.

They looked serious, dead serious, as they held their muskets at Matt and the other members of the club.

"Are we on television?" Hooter started to smile. "Is this *Totally Hidden Video*?"

"They speak queerly, sir. And their dress is foreign." An officer in the general's boat spoke up. "They could be spies."

The general nodded. "Where do you make your homes?" he asked.

"Rumson," Matt called back. "Rumson, Nebraska."

"Nebraska? Where is this place, Nebraska?" The general and his men looked perplexed, but the state of their confusion was nowhere near that of Matt and his friends.

"I never met anyone who didn't know where Nebraska was," Hooter mumbled through chattering teeth.

"Where . . . where do you think they're from?" Tony stammered.

"I don't know," Matt whispered, staring at the soldiers and their muskets. "But I have this strange feeling, like . . . like . . ."

"Like we've seen them someplace before," Q concluded.

"Where?" Hooter wanted to know. "Where have we seen them?"

"In our history book," Q whispered. "We've gone back in time!"

"You mean before TV and stuff?" Hooter asked,

looking at the old-fashioned muskets that were pointed at them.

"Before TV?" Q squeaked. His voice always turned into a series of squeaks when he was excited. "Try before electricity and flashlights. Try 1776 — the Revolutionary War!"

"That's why they don't know where Nebraska is," Matt exclaimed. "In 1776 there was no such state as Nebraska! How did this happen? And if we really have gone back in time, how are we going to get home?" Everyone stood staring at the boat full of ragged soldiers before them.

Tony turned to Matt. "You thought my backyard was so boring. I hope you're happy now."

Matt was too stunned to reply. It was true, the Adventure Club had been his idea, but he never dreamed it would turn out like this. Matt closed his eyes tight, wishing they could go back, back to the safety of a few hours ago, when his life had been normal and safe, and his biggest problem had been to finish the peas on his dinner plate!

Eight

MATT KEPT HIS EYES CLOSED, hoping it was all a bad dream, but when he finally opened them he knew he wasn't dreaming. He, Q, Tony, and Hooter were all awake, awake in the eighteenth century! Hooter was beginning to sniffle and the others fought to hold back tears.

"They are dressed in a queerish fashion but, have a look, General. They're just children," a young officer said, holding a lantern near Tony's face.

"That may be so," the general replied gravely. "But we mustn't underestimate the cowardly ingenuity of the enemy. They've been known to enlist babes as runners before." He motioned for one of his men to gather up the "runners." "God forgive the cold Tory heart that would send children out to face the dangers of this night," the general muttered, shaking his head.

A young soldier stepped into the old rowboat and

reached for Matt and Q first, grabbing them by the arms and directing them over to the general's vessel. He then tried to separate Hooter and Tony, but Hooter had pulled Tony to him and wouldn't let go. He was holding him to his chest as if Tony were his teddy bear. Actually Hooter still slept with a teddy bear but it was a secret he had kept from his friends. Tony wasn't furry or cuddly like his bear but Hooter wasn't about to be choosy. He was so scared he just needed something to hold on to.

"Hooter, let go! You're squeezing me so hard I can't breathe," Tony cried as they were lifted together onto the general's boat.

"Sorry," Hooter mumbled, without loosening his grip. Matt reached for Katie, who had called to him. The soldier placed her in his lap, covering her with the general's cape. She seemed to be dazed and promptly fell asleep in Matt's arms, worn out from her ordeal. Matt hugged her to him.

As the four boys sat huddled together, the oarsmen dressed in tattered blue and buff uniforms used their long poles to push off the ice. Matt recognized them from the history report he and Q had worked on together.

"They must be John Glover's Marbleheaders!" he whispered to Q.

"This must be the Delaware River," Q whispered back. Both boys remembered reading about the special group of seafaring enlisted men from the north, under the guidance of Colonel John Glover of Mar-

39

blehead, Massachusetts. They had manned the sturdy Durham boats that had carried Washington and his troops across the river on that Christmas night.

As a huge slab of ice crashed into the stern, Matt's eyes were riveted to the Marbleheader who stood in front of him. The sailor's freezing hands never left his oar as he worked to steady the stricken craft. The boat tipped dangerously to the left and the oarsman was almost thrown overboard. Suddenly the large hand of the general reached out for him and the oarsman regained his balance, thanking the general for his assistance.

"No, sir, it's you we owe our thanks to. Without your skill and that of your men this venture would surely be lost," General Washington told him. Matt found himself staring up at the famous man, who was suddenly standing beside him. He was taller than Matt had imagined, with huge hands. One hand held on to the side of the boat while the other rested on the shiny gold hilt of his sword. Matt couldn't resist. With his index finger he gently grazed the general's black boot.

I touched him! Matt thought. *I touched George Washington!* At that moment the general looked down.

"God willing, we'll all live to remember this night," the general whispered.

You will live to remember this, Matt thought to himself. *You will!* And it was then that he realized the amazing amount of courage that this man and those of his followers must have had, for they had no way of knowing if this dangerous expedition would succeed or fail. They hadn't studied the Revolutionary War in history last semester. Matt thought about the nine-mile hike to Trenton that the soldiers had yet to make, in order to surprise the Hessian mercenaries who were stationed there.

Matt looked around the boat at the rebel soldiers. Their uniforms, what was left of them, were threadbare. Many had no overcoats or hats. The snow was blowing from the northeast, and seemed to leave a layer of thin ice on the poorly clad soldiers. They shuddered and shivered and yet none complained. Matt's teeth were chattering as he looked over to Tony, who now seemed glad to have Hooter's big arms around him. Matt had never felt so cold, but as he curled his toes in his high-tops he noticed the soldier next to him. He was young, not more than sixteen or seventeen years old. The soldier had no jacket, just a loose linen overshirt, and instead of boots or shoes his feet were wrapped in rags. With one hand he held his musket and with the other he rubbed the frozen toes that stuck out of the bloody cloth wrapped around his foot. He was staring at Matt's sneakers.

Matt held on to Katie a little tighter and tried looking away. He knew his sneakers and down vest must seem strange to someone in the 1700s. He felt cowardly to be so well dressed. He knew the young soldier must be longing to have his feet in some dry shoes, and to have a warm coat. Matt lowered his head into his down vest as the snow blew about his face.

When he and Q had worked on their history report, Matt had read a great deal about the courage of the rebel soldiers fighting for the freedom of their country. He had imagined himself fighting alongside them, strong and courageous, charging the enemy line. But in his daydreams he had always been in a fine blue and white uniform. He never saw himself freezing and barefoot! He felt the young rebel's gaze upon him and when he looked up he was surprised to see the soldier smiling at him.

He seemed about to speak to Matt when a large ice floe next to them was suddenly broken up by the maneuverings of a long flat ferry carrying horses. The men on the ferry were trying to calm the frightened animals, who threatened to bolt into the river.

The noise of animals, men, and the crashing of ice was frightening. As the snow let up, Matt could see a line of boats and flat-topped ferries fighting their way across the icy river. It was then he remembered that all of Washington's 2,400 troops were ferried across the river on this Christmas night. He never dreamt that it would be such an undertaking and such a spectacle. Matt looked over to Q, who hadn't stopped adjusting his glasses since he came aboard. Hooter was still sitting with his arms wrapped around Tony.

As they came closer to the Jersey shore, Matt noticed an officer whispering to the young barefoot soldier. Matt knew he was an officer thanks to Q's yanking on his sleeve and pointing it out to him.

"Look at the paper in his hat," Q whispered excitedly. Matt grinned, remembering how they had given the oral part of their report wearing blue baseball caps with a piece of white paper taped to the brims. They had explained to the class how General Washington had ordered all of his officers to stick a piece of paper in their hats, so the men could recognize the officers in the dark.

Matt watched as the officer moved from the barefoot soldier and made his way to the general. The general seemed distracted and as the officer whispered in his ear General Washington's eyes were darting from boat to boat and then to the shore. He hardly seemed to give the officer any notice. Finally he looked down at Matt and Katie and shook his head. Matt watched as the officer made his way back to the young soldier and he heard his hushed command.

"The general agrees that if you have family and shelter nearby, it would be the safest place for the children. It would be too dangerous to let them disembark on the Jersey shore. Your orders are then to make the return voyage and take the children to McConkey's Inn for the night. From there you're to escort them to your family's home and keep watch over them until you've received further instructions.

These are dangerous times and the general's attention must be on the enemy. I'll trust you'll be able to set his mind at ease on this matter, Corporal Hibbs."

The soldier nodded. "Yes, sir."

"I'm entrusting you as their guardian and your reward will be warm feet tonight, lad." The officer smiled.

"I'll do my best, sir."

"Yes, Adam, I believe you will." The officer put his hand on Adam Hibbs's shoulder.

On hearing this, Hooter and Tony looked over to Matt and Q, and together all the members of the Adventure Club found themselves staring up at their new guardian, Adam Hibbs!

Nine

ADAM HIBBS! DID YOU HEAR that?" Q whispered in Matt's ear. "He's Adam Hibbs!"

Matt shot a glance at Tony and Hooter, who were both staring at the young rebel. Tony looked at Matt and his mouth dropped open. Matt tried to smile.

"If it's the same Adam Hibbs, then he'll know about the lake and the rowboat and he can tell us how to get back." Matt leaned over and whispered to his comrades.

"If that's the same Adam Hibbs," Q said, his voice beginning to go from a low whisper to a high squeak, "if that's the same Adam Hibbs, what's he still doing here?"

A cold, sobering feeling filled Matt's entire body. He looked back up at Adam Hibbs who nodded knowingly in his direction. The way the man stared at him, Matt was certain he was the same Adam Hibbs.

Before he had a chance to think any further on the subject, Matt's attention was diverted to another matter. They had finally reached the other side of the river and the long Durham boat was guided out of the tangle of ice and came to rest on solid ground.

There was an eerie quiet as the soldiers poured out of the boats, silently clutching their muskets. No words were spoken, no one dared break the stillness that ensured their safety. Even the horses had quieted down, glad to be off the water and little suspecting the dangerous ground they approached.

Matt knew that surprise was essential for their survival. He remembered reading that while the tough, professional German soldiers slept off a night of Christmas celebrations in Trenton, Washington's men would be creeping along the river and then turn inward to surprise the enemy, just as dawn broke.

As their boat emptied out, the boys stretched their legs. It had been a cramped voyage, for the boat had been filled to capacity before they came aboard. The last remaining soldier shook hands with Corporal Hibbs. Matt watched as the young rebel stood and hugged his fellow soldier good-bye.

"Godspeed, Thomas," Adam Hibbs whispered. Both soldiers looked to be about the same age and Matt wondered if they had been friends long. He imagined they had been through a great deal of hardship together for he could feel the sadness and fear at this parting. It was a parting all of them knew could well be their last.

Katie, who had slept through the entire voyage, suddenly turned in her sleep, throwing off part of the cape that covered her. Looking down, Matt remembered the general. *His cape! He'll need his cape,* Matt thought as he hurriedly unsnapped his down vest. He took off the vest and then lifted Katie out of the cape and into Q's arms. He shook the wet vest over the side of the boat and then wrapped it around Katie, trying to keep the dry side of the vest close to her. Then he turned to Adam Hibbs.

"The general forgot this," he said, holding the cape in his arms. "He'll need it for the march, won't he?"

Adam Hibbs frowned. All the soldiers had left the boat and the oarsmen that remained were given orders not to leave their craft. The young corporal knew that his responsibility was to guard over the children, but he also knew that the general should have his cape.

"All right, you take it to him, but straight away and don't tarry. I'll be keeping an eye on you from here," he warned. Matt looked back at Q, Tony, and Hooter. He couldn't believe his luck. He felt that in a way he was taking part in the Revolution. He was returning the mighty general's cape. He had been given the responsibility for keeping the father of our country from freezing! He climbed out of the boat feeling like a true rebel!

Matt was glad that he had worn his old hooded blue sweatshirt rather than the new red one his mother had wanted him to wear. *They would have thought I was a redcoat for sure,* he thought, making his way through the groups of soldiers that were on the shore. As he walked along, Matt noticed that each regiment seemed to have a different uniform, and they weren't all blue. There were soldiers in blue, green, brown, and beige coats. Some wore three-cornered hats, while others had round felt hats with feathers. Still others wore headbands with the words "Liberty or Death" stitched on them. He now understood why this new American Army was called "Washington's ragtag band of rebels."

However, in spite of their unprofessional look, Matt marveled at the soldiers' determination. Many of them wore only linen shirts, and pants that were tattered and frayed at the knees. A great number were in rags wrapped around their heads or legs and feet. In every group, two or three men stood coughing, their thin frames shaking, as they clutched their chests in pain. As Matt came close he could smell the sweat and dirt of clothing that hadn't been washed in weeks or months.

Yet even in these miserable conditions, Matt could feel the excitement in the air. The silence of the ragged rebel army could not conceal their hope and joy. They had trusted their leader, and he had not let them down. General Washington had gotten them across the treacherous Delaware, as he had promised, a feat the Hessian mercenaries would not even attempt. Matt could almost taste the rebels determination and he felt proud to be walking among them. He pretended that he was one of them, as he made his way up to a group of officers that were surrounding the general. He tried to inch his way into the huddle, when a large hand was suddenly on his neck.

"Just where would you be going now, lad?" a heavyset captain whispered. He was holding Matt by the back of his sweatshirt and had lifted him off of the ground.

"The general's cape. I'm . . . I'm to give him his cape," Matt sputtered.

"The general's busy conferring with his officers, but give it here and I'll see that he gets it," the captain said, reaching for the cape. He had thick wild eyebrows that were frozen in different directions, giving him the look of a madman. Matt didn't argue. He was about to turn and head back to the boat when the captain grabbed him by the arm.

"Come now, son. You don't look old enough to hold a musket. Just what regiment would you be with?" The captain had his face close to Matt's and Matt could smell his sour rum breath.

"Regiment? Um . . . I'm from the boat. I have to get back to the boat," Matt pleaded, trying to back away.

"No, we'll not be returning to the boats, tonight." The captain shook his head. "Tonight I'll wager we'll be sweeping those Hessian pigs off the streets of Trenton." He tightened his grip on Matt and was leading him away from the shore.

"But Corporal Hibbs! I'm to return to the boat with Corporal Hibbs!" Matt cried.

"Hush now, lad," the captain whispered, pulling Matt along. "This is no time for turning back. You wouldn't want to let the general down now, would you?"

"But . . ." Matt stammered.

"Hush now." The captain put his hand over Matt's mouth. As they passed a flatboat that was being unloaded on to the shore, the captain reached in and pulled out a musket and a cartridge box from a pile of guns. He shoved it into Matt's hands. "Aye, now, don't you look the rebel terror?" He laughed under his breath.

Matt felt the heavy weight of the musket in his hands. He looked down at the cold pointed spike of the bayonet and he was suddenly filled with terror. They couldn't think that he would know how to use it! This was all a mistake. He wasn't a rebel! He was just a kid from the twentieth century, who lived in a condo, and watched TV, and ate food that was cooked in a microwave. What did he know about bayonets and Hessian pigs? He turned his head, straining to see down the shoreline. Where was Adam Hibbs? Why hadn't he come after him?

The march to Trenton was to be a silent one. Many of the farmers and citizens along the Jersey side of the Delaware were known to be loyal to King George. If they were to stay alive, the rebels would have to make the nine-mile hike as soundlessly as they could. It was due to this enforced silence that word of the accident that befell a certain Corporal Hibbs never reached most men. As they marched noise-lessly over the frozen ground, most of his comrades were unaware that Adam Hibbs lay bleeding, with his head resting in Hooter Melrose's lap. It seems the young corporal had been standing in a boat looking up the shore when he stumbled and fell onto his bayonet. They had sent him back across the river with the children to McConkey's Inn. A Corporal Neeley accompanied them, as Adam Hibbs was not expected to live the night.

But Matthew Carlton knew none of this. All he knew was that he had somehow gotten himself into what had once been just a daydream. He was a rebel soldier in the middle of the Revolutionary War. Only now that the daydream had come true it seemed more like a nightmare!

Ten

THEY'RE GOING TO WALK *all the way to Trenton! Nine miles! I'll never be able to walk nine miles in this storm. I'm freezing.* Matt curled his half-frozen fingers around the musket. He had taken the cartridge box and put the strap over his head, wearing it under his arm, as he had seen the other soldiers do. Without his down vest the wind seemed to cut right through him. His nose had begun to run and wouldn't stop. His toes ached with the cold inside of his sneakers. He thought about turning around and trying to run, but he was afraid that he would be taken for a spy, or worse yet, a coward.

Where is Adam Hibbs? he wondered. *And what will Katie think when she wakes up without me? I wonder if I'll ever see her or the guys again. I've got to get back to them, but how?*

His thoughts were suddenly interrupted by Captain McCowly, who, after giving the cape to one of the general's aides, had stopped at a fencerow. A group of soldiers were pulling down the rails and had begun to build small fires to keep from freezing, when the captain ordered them to stop. "There will be no fires," he commanded. The men took the boards and used them to sit on instead. Many of the soldiers slept as they sat upright, while some took to whispering, their voices lost in the howling wind.

Matt laid his musket on the ground and began pulling on a board, but it wouldn't budge. He felt embarrassed by his weak attempts to pry the board loose. Finally a young rebel in rags leaned over and helped him to pull it free. Both he and Matt fell backwards as the board came loose in their hands.

They quickly got up and carried the board to a clearing. In silence, they sat down beside one another, hugging their knees to their chests to keep warm.

The young soldier couldn't have been more than fourteen or fifteen years old, yet there were dark circles under his eyes, giving him a haggard look of exhaustion. His face was blotchy with a rash that seemed to spread up from his neck. He was just about to close his eyes when he noticed Matt's footwear. With a quizzical look he inched closer and touched Matt's sneaker. Matt watched as the long fingernails caked with dirt lightly traced the red letters on his ankle.

"Reeboks," Matt whispered.

"Redcoats?" The young rebel quickly removed his hand.

"No, not redcoats. These are Reeboks. You know, sneakers."

"Sneakers?" The rebel looked wary.

"Oh, I guess you don't know. They're special shoes made of rubber," Matt whispered. But the soldier didn't seem to understand. He surveyed Matt's sweatshirt and jeans.

"Where are you from?" he asked. "This dress is foreign to me and not of any colony I know."

Matt remembered from his history report that in 1776 each colony still had a separate style of dress, and you could often tell a New York regiment from a regiment of Virginia rebels simply by the color shirts they wore. He also knew that Nebraska was not yet a colony in 1776. He paused, thinking about his aunt Shelly and uncle Mark.

"Well, I have relatives living in Maryland," he said truthfully. The young rebel nodded, seeming to accept this.

"My name is Israel Gates, and truth be known I've never been to Maryland and I've never seen such queer dress. But queer though it be, I would offer a trade for one of those snakers."

"Sneakers," Matt corrected.

"Aye, whatever you be calling them. I would give my shirt for one. It's right warm," he whispered, offering a raggedy sleeve for Matt to feel.

"But why trade your shirt for one shoe?" Matt didn't understand until Israel unwrapped the rags that bound his left foot. By the light of the moon, Matt could see the long gash that ran along the side of Israel's foot. It was puffy with infection and crusted with dirt. The whole foot seemed to be turning bluish-green.

"The pain of the wound has stopped. It's all numb, and though I'm glad for that, I'm afraid it's freezing up on me," Israel told him. Matt bit down on his lower lip at the sight of the foot, and quickly untied his sneaker. Israel began to lift his coat over his head. Matt could see that it was nothing more than an old blanket with a slit at the top and some crude stitching along the sides.

"No, keep your shirt," Matt whispered. "I'm warm enough." He took off his sneaker and sock and offered them to Israel.

"What kind of stockings are these?" Israel asked, feeling the soft cotton while peering down at the green stripes that went around the top of the sock. Matt couldn't help but smile.

"Nerd socks, that's what my friend Tony calls them. He won't wear any socks that have stripes." Israel gave Matt a strange look on hearing this and Matt suddenly realized the luxurious life he had left behind, where you could refuse to wear a sock just because it had stripes!

Israel put his foot in the sneaker with some difficulty, though he did get it in. Matt breathed a sigh of relief. "Thanks, Dad," he muttered under his breath, for his mother had always said that he got his big feet from his father's side of the family. Matt suddenly thought of his father and mother and tears came to his eyes, as he wondered if he would ever see them again.

"What did you say?" Israel asked.

"Oh, I was just thinking how glad I was for once that I have such big feet for a kid," Matt said, wiping a tear from his cheek.

"A goat?" Israel frowned.

"No, where I come from we call boys 'kids.' Like I would be a regular kid and you're older so you would be a big kid," Matt tried to explain.

Israel cocked his head and smiled slowly. "Where I come from they'd be calling you a sight dim for telling a man with a musket that he's an old goat!"

Matt was about to explain further when he saw that Israel was laughing. "I guess it does sound funny," Matt laughed as he quickly undid his other sneaker. He took off his one sock and put it on his left foot and then replaced the sneaker on his right foot. Matt knew that he would have to keep both feet covered to keep them from freezing. He knew it wouldn't be long before his sock became wet from stepping on ice and snow, and he wondered if he would have the courage that Israel had to keep going. Israel saw the worried look on his face and silently leaned over and began to wrap Matt's left foot in the dirty linen strips that had once been around his own foot. When he was through, both boys stretched out their legs and grinned.

"I don't know your name," Israel whispered, reaching into his haversack.

"Matt, uh, Matthew Carlton," Matt said shyly.

"Well, Matthew Carlton, you've been a good friend to me and I'll not forget it. Here, have some of this," he said, offering Matt what looked like a burnt piece of meat. Matt was starving and gratefully accepted the gift.

"Um . . . it's good. What is it?" he asked with a mouthful.

"Pigeon," Israel replied. "I trapped one a few days before we crossed the river. I'm glad I had enough time to roast him."

Pigeon? I'm eating pigeon! Matt thought with a grimace.

Israel reached down and took up a handful of snow to his mouth. "Would that we had a small beer to wash it down with, now there would be a feast."

"Um, a real feast," Matt said limply. *Would that we had a Coke and a hamburger, with a side of fries, now that would be a feast,* Matt thought to himself as he brought some snow to his mouth.

"It won't be long before I'll be eating regular meals again, and if we live through the next six days I shall return your gift in kind," Israel told him, trying to warm his hands with his breath. "My enlistment comes due the first of the year and with my wages I can pay for the nerd stocking and shoe."

"Don't worry about it," Matt whispered. "But what will you do when your enlistment is up? Will you sign up again and stay and fight?"

Israel closed his eyes and shook his head wearily. "This regiment is the twelfth of Massachusetts and I don't know that many of us could reenlist even if we wanted to. We barely got out of Montreal alive, what with the Indians and then the pox. The march to Albany killed off most of our wounded and sick, and this last march to Pennsylvania took still more. Those of us left have barely enough strength to lift our muskets. And tell me, what good will these be?" he said, reaching for his gun. "They're soaked after all this rain and snow and it will surely be a miracle to get them firing. At least you have a bayonet." He pointed to Matt's musket.

"Oh, I know there are those that are in high spirits because we seem to be on the offense at last, but I'll wager you won't find much cheer here. I've seen so much hardship that you could make me a general and I wouldn't reenlist. No." He sighed. "I've had enough of army life. All I want now is to get back to Massachusetts and a warm bed and a slice of hunter's pie. And besides, I've got to deliver these." He pulled out a small leather pouch from his pack and a dozen glass beads fell into his outstretched palm. "Aren't they fine?" he whispered as the light of the moon bounced off the delicate painted glass. "They'll make one pretty necklace." He smiled.

"They are pretty," Matt agreed. "Who do you have to deliver them to?"

"To one very demanding lady." Israel's blue eyes seemed to twinkle as he said this.

"Oh," Matt mumbled. "Like a girlfriend?"

"Girlfriend? Well, yes, she is a girl and surely a friend and also the fairest maid in Massachusetts. She's got a mop of gold curls and the face of an angel, though truth be telling, she's got a devil of a temper. When she's vexed with you, she'll stamp her feet and shake her little fists. She's something to contend with, I'll guarantee."

Matt moved closer to Israel. He wasn't much interested in hearing about girlfriends but he was glad for the company, no matter what they talked about. *Maybe,* he thought to himself, *with Israel for a friend, I'll be able to get through this march.* A chilling wind swept across the clearing and Matt hugged his knees even closer to his chest. "What's your girlfriend's name?" Matt asked with a shiver.

Israel smiled. "Abby, but I call her 'my gabby Abby.'" He laughed. "Not five years old and she can outtalk a tinker on a Monday!"

"Five years old?" Matt looked perplexed.

"Aye, she's my little sister." Israel smiled, wiping his nose on his sleeve. "My mother died in birthing her and since I was the eldest I promised my mum that I would watch over the little ones. My father

59

has a likeness for rum, you see. He spends most of his day in the tavern."

"Well, then, who's looking after Abby, now?" Matt asked.

"My brothers," Israel told him. "Ben is twelve years, Simon is eleven, and Nathan is eight. They're good boys but surely I hated to leave them alone . . . ." Israel's voice trailed off as he gazed up into the moon.

"It must have been hard for you to choose," Matt whispered.

"Choose?" Israel's eyebrows shot up.

"You know, choose between your family and your country. It's what a soldier has to do, I guess. Make his country safe for his family, right?"

Israel shook his head and gave a low sarcastic laugh. His voice became a husky whisper. "I don't know about you, but I thought these colonies were safe enough without a war. I had no desire to be a soldier and I wouldn't be here now if my father hadn't drank up what little coin he managed to bring in from his tailoring. I had to keep my promise to my mother, so it was up to me to see that we didn't starve. I sold the only thing I could and come December thirty-first my debt is paid."

"I don't understand," Matt whispered.

Israel studied his young friend's face. "You remind me of my brother Simon: bright eyes and thick head!" He sighed. "I sold myself as a substitute for a wealthy silversmith in Boston. I took on his enlistment papers in return for a cow and enough coin to keep my sister and brothers fed till spring. I only planned to stay till the enlistment was up, but when I found myself marching on foot in Montreal with a party of Indians fast on our heels, I decided to re-enlist so I could get home under the army's protection, and besides they were paying six dollars a month. Now I have just six more days to go and I can head home." He closed his eyes and smiled. Then he opened his hand and looked down at the beads again.

"I promised Abby a present, and so when we came across a tinker on the road to Albany I asked to see his wares. As soon as I saw these, I knew Abby would love them. Blue is her favorite color," he said, turning the beads over in his hand. "They come from France, you know. The tinker told me so." He grinned. "My lieutenant was right vexed with me for spending my last pistoreens on pretties. He scolded me for not buying some leather that I could have made up into some decent shoes. But I promised Abby I'd bring her back the prettiest present I could find and it was my last bit of coin. Many a tinker and shopkeeper won't take the paper we're paid. They don't believe the Continental currency is worth anything. But then you must know that. Though in truth you don't look old enough to count your wages much less earn them. How did you come to enlist?"

"Um . . ." Matt squirmed, trying not to look at

Israel. "The truth is I didn't enlist and you're right, I'm not old enough. It was an accident. You see, I got separated from my friends and sister. I have a little sister, too. Her name is Katie. Anyway, I was sleeping at a friend's house and I thought we could have an adventure and so we went for this walk after my friend's parents went to sleep and then . . ." His voice was beginning to crack as he tried to hold back the tears. "I don't know how this happened, how we ended up here. I never knew it would be like this. I'm not from here, Israel, you have to believe me. I'm from another — "

"It's all right," Israel interrupted him, leaning over and putting his arm around him. "I'll look after you. We two goats, we'll get through this together, you'll see, and when my enlistment is up we'll find your Katie and you and she can come and visit me and Abby and the boys. Don't worry, Matthew Carlton, you've got a friend in Israel Gates. You can depend on it."

Eleven

I'VE GOT A FRIEND. *I'll be all right. I'll be all right,* Matt told himself as he sat next to Israel, who had fallen asleep with his arm over Matt's shoulder. Matt tried closing his eyes but he was too frightened to sleep as he watched the soldiers that were gathering on the shore.

Matt hadn't spent much time away from home, except for summer visits to his grandparents, and even then his parents had called him on the phone every other day to see how he was doing. He closed his eyes now and imagined that he was talking to his mother on the phone.

"Oh, hi, Mom. How are you? Me? Oh, I'm great. I'm just hanging out in the eighteenth century. Behave myself? Don't worry, Mom, George Washington and a few of his friends are here to see to that. Home? I don't know when I'll be back, but I will come back, I promise."

But what if he couldn't get back? How would his parents feel with both their children missing? Matt began to imagine his mother's face as she looked into their bedrooms at night, only to find their beds empty.

"I'll get back, don't worry, Mom. Somehow I'll figure a way, and I will get back" Matt said as he hugged his knees to his chest.

For the first time in his life Matt was glad he had done his homework. If he hadn't done that history report, he probably wouldn't even know where he was right now.

He looked to his left and saw a group of soldiers unloading a large cannon. He noticed that they were all dressed in the same uniforms, with blue coats, dirty buff pants, and blue stockings. Most of them were wearing black three-cornered hats. They had ropes and hatchets tied to white straps that criss-crossed their chests. A dozen men had rolled the cannon off of the boat and were trying to pull it onto the shore.

Suddenly a large heavyset officer approached. Matt could tell that he was an officer of high rank from his ornate uniform and sword.

"Major Crane," the officer bellowed in a deep voice. "Have the three-pounders come ashore yet?"

"No," the major answered. "We've been waiting for them."

"There will be another scow crossing. They should be on it," the colonel told him. "Go easy on the men, John. They've a good piece of work to do yet," he said, nodding to the group of soldiers who were dragging the cannon.

"Yes, sir, Colonel Knox," the major replied.

Matt couldn't believe his ears. *It's Henry Knox! It's really him!* he thought excitedly. Matt had written three whole pages of his history report on the remarkable feats of Henry Knox and the men of his artillery division. He watched as the huge Colonel Knox directed another group of soldiers in the unloading of some smaller guns.

So that's what the bookseller from Boston looks like, Matt thought, smiling to himself. He remembered reading how the two-hundred-and-eighty-pound Henry had turned his bookstore in Boston over to his brother so that he could join up and fight the British. Henry Knox was a patriot at heart and couldn't bear to see his country under the unfair rule of King George.

He was smart and strong and full of spirit, and so even though he lacked experience, Henry Knox was given command of the Continental Artillery Regiment. He had led an expedition all the way up to Fort Ticonderoga in order to round up some big guns, much needed in the Boston siege. Overcoming incredible obstacles, he had led his men back three hundred miles to Boston, dragging some fifty cannons, howitzers, and mortars on ox-drawn sledges. Matt remembered reading that, without Henry Knox and his artillery, many a battle would have been lost. Matt also knew that General Washington was depending on these remaining eighteen guns for his attack on Trenton.

As Matt sat watching, he saw General Washington approach Colonel Knox and Major Crane. Henry Knox looked at the general and shook his head.

"We're hours behind with this damn storm," he muttered. "It will surely be daybreak before we can reach the town."

General Washington looked out across the river. "Yes, this storm works against us," he said, frowning. "And yet it may work with us, for if this turbulence continues, God granting, the day will be dark."

"It's a miracle we haven't lost a boat yet, with all this ice." Major Crane sighed. "If we could only expedite the crossing," he complained.

"Patience, John, patience," the general whispered, placing his hand on the young officer's shoulder.

It was a gesture that reminded Matt of his own father. Just last Saturday night they had stood that way out in their backyard. Matt remembered how impatiently he had been waiting for a hamburger as his father stood cooking them over the grill.

"Hang on, champ," Mr. Carlton had chided, while Matt shifted from foot to foot impatiently. "We've got to let this cow cook a bit," his father laughed, putting his hand on Matt's shoulder. "You've just got to learn to be more patient, Matt."

66

If only you could see me now, Dad, Matt thought sleepily. *You wouldn't believe how patient I've become, sitting here waiting for George Washington to lead me into battle!*

As Matt fell asleep he began to dream of being at home in his backyard with his family. He felt safe and warm and at peace.

Colonel Knox suddenly appeared in the dream saying, "Come on now, lads, hurry up, hurry up . . ." The colonel's voice was suddenly getting louder as Matt began to wake up.

"Hurry up, hurry up now, lads," the colonel called, nudging Matt and then Israel. Matt rubbed his eyes in confusion.

"Dad?" Matt said sleepily.

"We won't be seeing your dad today, lad. Come along, we've got to catch up to General Greene's patrol. Hurry now, on your feet," a deep voice called.

Matt opened his eyes and found Captain McCowly standing before him. He blinked hard, feeling as if he were waking from one dream into another. As Matt stood up he noticed that Israel had slumped over beside him. He was still asleep. "Israel?" Matt shook him gently. "We've got to go now," Matt whispered.

Israel opened his eyes, but it took a long while for him to fully wake up, and he seemed to have a hard time standing. "Are you okay?" Matt asked, helping him to his feet.

"Okay?" Israel shook his head. "What is an okay?" he asked in a weak voice.

"All right. Are you all right? You don't look so good, old goat," Matt said softly.

Israel smiled weakly. "And you've got the mug of King George's horse. Now help me with my pack, will you, Master Bright Eyes?"

"Sure," Matt whispered, helping him to lift his pack onto his back. They walked side by side in a line with four other soldiers. With each step Matt felt the full fury of the storm as the wind ripped through the trees sending icy branches across the road. Up ahead they could just make out the dim glow of a lantern that one of the soldiers was carrying. The light flickered faintly as the snow threatened to extinguish the flame. Matt felt like he was in the middle of a hurricane. The snow mixed with sleet cut into his face and he buried his head in his sweatshirt. When he did steal a glance at the other men, Matt could see that they were all moving forward, with heads lowered, following almost blindly the steps of those before them.

As Matt trudged along, looking neither to the left or the right, he thought about these soldiers. He knew that for security's sake most of the men knew nothing of their destination. For many it was enough to know that they were ridding the colonies of the tyrannical rule of King George and the heavy taxes he had imposed on them. He thought about men like Henry Knox, who believed in freedom and were willing to give up their lives for that cause. And yet for others, like Israel, six dollars a month was enough to bring them into the face of battle.

"Six dollars," Matt muttered as a sharp stone cut into his linen-bound foot. *I could spend that much in six minutes at the mall! Not that there is a mall anywhere near here,* he thought gloomily, looking into the darkened woods. *What I wouldn't give to see a mall right now, with heat and electric lights and restaurants and shoe stores! But that's all two hundred years away. I've got to figure out a way to get us home,* he thought, stepping through an icy puddle. *I wish I was home. I wish I was home right now.*

Twelve

MATT HAD NEVER EXPERIENCED such a storm. He couldn't even remember the last time he had been out in the rain and, when he finally did remember, he realized it was just to run a few feet from the car to the store.

What I wouldn't give for a ride in a nice big heated car, he thought. *And it wouldn't even have to have a radio.* He wiped at his nose, which had begun to run again, and he began to wonder if his body would ever stop hurting. He was trying to figure out which part hurt most, his chapped face or his frozen fingers, when he suddenly felt the cold ice seeping into his linen-bound foot. He groaned with each step that left his foot a little wetter. But he kept his groans as low as he could and hoped they wouldn't be heard over the wind.

When he looked at Israel, Matt saw his friend's head bent down into his chest. The rags that Israel had wrapped around the top of his head were frozen and the snow was beginning to pile up on them, so that he looked as if he were wearing a white cap. Every now and then Israel would stop, as a fit of coughing overtook him. Matt would wait beside him, not knowing how to help him.

Matt tried looking around to see where they were, but it was all a blur of snow and trees. They could have been walking in circles for all he knew. After they had marched for what seemed like hours, the low voice of an officer called for them to halt. As Matt stood in line, a group of officers rode up beside him on horseback. Israel reached out and pulled Matt from the edge of the road, for one horse had nearly stepped on Matt's foot. Together the two friends silently watched as the group of officers held a short meeting. Matt and Israel could just make out the conversation.

"Our orders are to break the detachment into two divisions," a burly-looking lieutenant was explaining. "General Sullivan will lead the march along the River Road and General Washington and General Greene will take a column along the Pennington Road. The distance both divisions are traveling is roughly the same. Upon forcing the out-guards, you're to push directly into the town, that we may charge the enemy before they have time to form. His Excellency is determined that our destiny be decided this night. He beseeches you to instill in your men the necessity to bring down every Hessian until Trenton is freed of their scourge, for if we find defeat here, Philadelphia is surely lost."

"So, that's it," Israel whispered to Matt as the officer rode off. "I knew when they ordered three days' rations that we were up for some endeavor. It's the Hessians in Trenton, is it? Have you ever seen one of those giants?"

"Giants? What do you mean, giants?" Matt gulped.

"I've heard that most are as tall as three men," Israel told him, rocking in place. Matt began rocking also, for it seemed too painfully cold to stand still for any length of time.

"They're sent straight from hell," a stocky drummer who was standing in their line whispered. "They wear their hair down to their waists like barbarians and they take no quarters."

"No quarters?" Matt looked over to Israel.

"Henry Schudder, this is Matthew Carlton. Matthew's new to this army life," Israel explained with a cough. "What Henry means is no mercy, Matthew. The Hessians would sooner run you through with their bayonets than have to look at you. They're mercenaries, you see. Paid to kill and come all the way from Hessia to do it. You can bet they didn't know a patriot from a Tory till they landed here."

"They don't care who their victims be, just as long as there is gold in their pockets," Henry added. "Oh, this camp itch has me legs so raw that me breeches are stuck fast," he moaned, pulling at his pants.

"Do you really think they're that bad?" Matt whispered, trying to keep the trembling out of his voice.

"Me legs? Aye, the blazing itch has spread straight to me shins," Henry groaned.

But Israel noticed Matt's worried look. "You just stay close to me, little goat." He smiled. "Together we'll take care of those Hessians. We're a team," he said, his voice breaking into another cough.

"When we come up against that bloodthirsty lot, you'll be needing more than Master Gates, here," Henry grumbled. He looked down and adjusted the strap that held his drum. Matt was suddenly curious.

"Henry, why is your coat red? Isn't that the color of the enemy?" Matt wanted to know.

Henry Schudder cocked his head and smirked. "You are new to army life aren't you?" He shook his head. "Just how old are you, anyway?" he asked.

"Ten . . . uh ten and a half, really," Matt answered, trying to sound as old as he could.

"I suppose that explains it." The freckle-faced Henry sighed. And it seemed a very mature sigh to Matt, who didn't know that Henry was just three years older than he.

"I'm the drummer for my regiment, so my colors are reversed. Our company wears blue jackets with red facings, so my coat is red with blue facings," Henry explained.

"An officer has got to pick out his drummer in battle, to give the signals," Israel told Matt. "It's often so hard to see, what with cannon fire and gun smoke, that it would take too long to go looking for a face, so the drummer is in opposite colors and can be recognized that easy." Just as he finished his explanation, Israel was seized with another fit of coughing. He had been coughing from the beginning of the march but had kept his head low in his coat to muffle the sound.

Matt turned and looked behind him. The snow had let up, and as far back as he could see there were soldiers and artillery on the road. The view from the front was the same. He suddenly felt trapped. There could be no turning back now. He would actually have to face those "bloodthirsty" Hessians. Matt stood shivering and wondering what they would really be like. He knew that the Americans had won the battle at Trenton but he didn't know how many rebels were killed in the attack. He seemed to remember from his report that there were only a few casualties. Matt felt a sudden wave of terror come over him, as he realized he could now be one of those few!

Thirteen

I WONDER HOW KATIE IS DOING? Matt was thinking as he shook some snow from his head. *I hope she's warm, and I hope she's safe. I'll never forgive myself if anything happens to her.*

Matt frantically looked down at his musket as he tried to figure out how to load it. His shoulders tensed as he thought of the overwhelming task before him.

On turning to look at his friend, Matt was horrified to find Israel stooped over on the ground, groaning.

"Israel!" Matt cried, kneeling down beside him. "Israel, what is it? What's wrong?"

But Israel didn't answer. He was on his knees, bracing himself with one hand on the ground, and with the other he reached for Matt's arm. His body suddenly went rigid as he began to violently throw up. Matt turned his head away, embarrassed, and not knowing how to help his friend.

When Israel finally exhausted himself, he loosened his grip on Matt's arm. Israel sank back on the ground, trembling. He slowly lifted his head and Matt winced at the sight of phlegm and blood dripping from Israel's mouth.

"Forward on." The call was given to continue the march. Matt and Henry helped Israel to his feet. He could barely stand, and weaved unsteadily, as he tried to put one foot in front of the other.

"Lean on me, Israel," Matt whispered, coming close beside him. Together the two of them kept up as best they could. The pace was extremely slow due to the storm and the poor condition of the road. As Matt looked down, he could see the bloodied snow, left by the bare feet of those who had gone before him.

After what seemed like hours of marching, Matt could feel the full weight of Israel's body. He suddenly realized that Israel had given up trying to walk at all.

"Henry, help!" Matt called, for he and Israel had begun to topple over. Henry reached over and grabbed Israel's arm and together he and Matt tried dragging him along. They hadn't gone far when Israel sank to his knees again, pulling them down.

Matt and Henry got to their feet just as an officer rode by on horseback. "Move him to the side of the road," the officer ordered, on seeing Israel slumped over in another fit of retching and coughing. As they dragged him off the road, Matt felt something hot on his hand. He looked down and was horrified to see that it was some of the blood that his friend was bringing up. Wiping his hand in the snow, Matt cringed with the thought that it was the first bit of warmth he had felt for hours.

Israel was suddenly quiet. The spasms had stopped but this time he didn't try to stand.

"Come on, Israel, I'll help you," Matt offered.

But Israel smiled weakly and shook his head. "You'll have to go on without me," he said hoarsely.

"Oh, no, Israel. You can make it. You can lean on me," Matt cried. "We've got to take care of those Hessians together, remember? We're a team."

"Let him be," Henry whispered, pulling Matt away. "There's enough here to take care of the Hessians. Israel's fighting is over. Let him be."

"But . . . but we can't leave him here alone!" Matt was incredulous. "He'll freeze to death!"

"He'll go to his reward either way," Henry told him. "Better to let him out of his agony now than to drag him along any further. Come on now. We've got to catch up to the regiment."

"I won't. I can't," Matt said, fighting back the tears. "He's my friend."

"And friends die!" Henry shouted, grabbing onto the front of Matt's sweatshirt and shaking him hard. "And you'll die, too, if you stay here with him in this storm. You're sure to freeze to death. Don't you see?"

But Matt wouldn't listen. He pulled himself away and knelt down beside Israel.

"Stay here then, you little fool," Henry called, exasperated. "But if you change your mind just get back on the road and follow it till you find us. And whatever you do, don't fall asleep or you'll never waken." He stood shaking his head, and unwrapping the wool strips that he had wrapped around his hands. He threw them to Matt and in a brusque voice said, "Wrap these around yourself and you may save a few fingers."

Matt watched as he unbuttoned the blue cuffs on his coat and pulled them down over his own bare knuckles. Then without another word, Henry Schudder turned and ran until he finally disappeared into the long stream of soldiers that moved along the road.

Matt put his arm around Israel, who seemed to be dozing. He wondered if Israel even knew he was with him. As the steady line of men marched past, Matt grew panicky with fear. He longed to call out to them to stop and take him with them. He saw that most of them had their heads lowered and didn't even notice him, and those that did gave him a mournful nod and quickly looked away.

I wish we were going with them, Matt thought, now jealous of those on their way to battle. *At least we would have had a chance. What chance do we have here?*

He was suddenly overcome with the strong ammonia scent of urine. Looking down he could see that Israel had wet himself and didn't even seem to know it. Matt took the rags that Henry had thrown him and laid them over Israel's wet pants. It was all he could think to do. His eyes filled with tears as he realized just how helpless Israel had become and how desperate their situation was because of it.

Maybe Henry was right, he thought. *Maybe friends do die but that doesn't mean that you have to die with them. Maybe he won't even miss me,* Matt thought, looking at Israel's closed eyes. "I don't want to die. I want to live. I want to live!" he whispered.

Slowly taking his arm from around Israel, Matt reached over and picked up his musket. He stood up and was about to join the soldiers filing past, when Israel suddenly opened his eyes and smiled.

"Go on then, Matthew. Go on ahead. It's all right. I'm just going to take a little nap," he said, curling up on the frozen ground.

Matt's musket fell from his hands as he sank back in the snow. "No, Israel, stay awake. You've got to stay awake," he cried, pulling his friend up against a tree. Israel blinked and his eyes met Matt's.

"Don't worry, old goat," Matt said, holding him in his arms. "I'm here with you. I'm not going anywhere," he whispered softly. Then with his half-frozen fingers he brushed the snow from Israel's cheek.

"My pouch," Israel said faintly. "Can you get it for me? It's in my pack." Matt reached into the pack on Israel's back and pulled out the small leather pouch.

"The beads, put them in my hand so I can see them, will you?" Israel asked.

"Sure," Matt replied, opening the bag. Then he uncurled Israel's half-frozen fist. The fingers had become blistered and were turning purple with the cold. Matt held the pouch upside down and carefully shook it. On seeing the pretty blue beads, Israel smiled.

"They are fine, aren't they?" He sighed.

Matt looked down at the delicate little beads that were so gently cradled in the dirty frozen hand.

"Very fine," Matt whispered.

"Promise me, Matthew, that you'll get them to her," Israel said, struggling to keep his head up. "Miss Abigail Gates, on the Dinberry Road, Haverston, Massachusetts." He slumped back down out of breath.

"What are you talking about?" Matt wiped at the tears falling from his cheek. "Of course she'll get them. We're going to bring them to her together, remember. You did invite Katie and me to come and visit you and Abby and the boys. We're going to bring Abby the beads together, Israel, we are."

But Israel shook his head weakly as his breathing became more labored. "Please promise me," he gasped.

"I promise, I promise," Matt said, pulling him to his chest. "Miss Abigail Gates, on the Dinberry Road,

Haverston, Massachusetts. Don't worry, Israel Gates, you have a friend in Matthew Carlton," he whispered softly as the tears on his face began to freeze. "You can depend on it."

Israel could no longer speak, but Matt could feel him thanking him with his eyes. Matt put the beads in his sweatshirt pocket, keeping his other arm around his friend. They sat huddled together like that for a long time. The steady stream of soldiers passing before them began to blur as Matt's field of vision narrowed. The howling of the wind seemed to lessen and an enticing quiet crept over the landscape as the snow silently encased the two comrades in its frozen cocoon.

Matt felt his eyes beginning to close and to help him fight the urge to sleep he began to talk. He told Israel all about himself and his life in the future. Israel seemed to be going in and out of consciousness as Matt rattled on about dirt bikes, VCR's, and pizza.

"And, oh, yeah, Batman. I've got to tell you about Batman. See, there's this guy, Bruce Wayne, who's living in Gotham City . . . are you listening, Israel?"

Fourteen

AKE UP! WAKE UP, son. Come now, it's no time for sleeping." Matt could hear a deep voice calling. It sounded as if it were coming from the end of a tunnel. He groaned as the voice got louder.

"I'm getting up, Dad. I am," Matt mumbled, with his eyes still closed. "Tell Mom I don't want any breakfast. I've got gym first period today and I'll just throw up if I have to eat anything," he moaned.

"I'm glad to hear that you still have enough life in you to be talking about breakfast," the deep voice replied. "There you are, on your feet."

Matt opened his eyes and found himself standing, or rather leaning on a heavyset man in a brown wool cloak. He was an older man, with bushy gray eyebrows and a bristly mustache.

"Dad? Is that you, Dad?" Matt croaked.

The man smiled, shaking the snow from Matt's

head. "No, lad, I'm not your father. My name is Nathan Hornbee. You're just a bit confused, is all. Come on then, you need to thaw out and get some of that breakfast you were groaning about. My farm is just through these woods, not an hour's ride. We can take my Bess, here," he said, walking Matt to his horse.

Matt blinked hard and suddenly realized where he was. "Israel," he called out. "My friend is sick," he said, turning to face Mr. Hornbee. "You've got to help me with him," Matt pleaded. He looked behind him, searching for Israel.

But Mr. Hornbee quickly turned him around. "No, lad, don't look back there," he said, keeping his large gloved hands on Matt's shoulders. "I'm afraid there's nothing more to be done for your friend now."

"But I can't leave him!" Matt protested, wriggling out of the old man's grasp and running from him. When Matt reached the tree, he let out a sound that was half-cry and half-scream, for there lying on his back was Israel. Matt knew it was Israel because he could see the bit of blue from the old coat that stuck out of the snow, and the bright red sneaker, with its frozen laces all undone. There was little else to recognize, for the storm had left its gruesome mark, erasing Israel's face in a cover of snow.

"I can't leave him. I can't," Matt sobbed.

"Aye, lad, you can," Mr. Hornbee said, gently. "For he's left himself. He's no longer here, but in

God's glorious kingdom." The old man put his arm around Matt and guided him to the horse.

"The patriots are just down this road," Mr. Hornbee whispered. "There are Tories living all through these parts and if Colonel Rall is alerted, these woods will be crawling with Hessian Jagers and rebel hunters. We must make haste." But Matt was so exhausted and overcome with grief that he began to topple over. He remembered little of Mr. Hornbee's lifting him onto his horse or the ride to the Hornbee farm.

When Matt finally came to his senses, it was his sense of smell that came alive first. He sniffed the sweet aroma of wood smoke and apples. On opening his eyes, he found himself lying before a large fireplace. Several black cast-iron pots and kettles hung from an iron arm that swung out over the fire. In the pot closest to Matt, a brew of spicy apple cider was slowly simmering.

Matt yawned, lazily savoring the delicious feeling of warmth that had spread over him. The bitter cold and dampness of the night before seemed far away as Matt snuggled down under the cozy mountain of wool blankets that had been piled on him. It was such a relief to feel good, finally, that he decided not to think about it, and to just feel it. But as soon as he decided not to think about it he couldn't stop thinking about it.

Why do I feel so good? Matt wondered. *And where am I?* Looking down beneath the blankets, he could see that he was no longer in his clothes. Instead he had on a long white nightgown with ruffles around the collar and cuffs. He winced, instinctively knowing that it was a woman's garment.

As Matt looked around, he could see that the room was not very big, with one small window affording the only light. Matt looked out the window and saw that it was an overcast day. He wondered what time it was. He looked past the window to see a long narrow table with some wooden bowls on it. In a corner there was a spinning wheel. A basket overflowing with raw wool sat beside it.

In another corner a woman was sitting at a loom. She was dressed very plainly in long skirts and a white apron. The expression on her face was as drab as the green-colored shawl that she wore over her shoulders. Her gray hair was pulled back tight in an angry little bun and the only sound that she made was the *wack wack wack* of her loom. Every now and then she would stop to nervously scratch at a scab on her face.

Mrs. Pritchet! Matt thought on seeing her. *She looks just like crabby old Mrs. Pritchet from the second grade!*

Suddenly the woman looked up, and on seeing Matt awake, her thin lips curled down into a frown. She dropped the shuttle from her hand and rushed from the room. Matt could hear her shrill tinny voice.

"Nathan! Nathan, he's awake!" she cried.

"Calm down, Temperance. He's only a child. He'll

bring us no harm," whispered Mr. Hornbee, coming into the room.

"His being here is harm enough," snapped the old woman angrily behind him.

Mr. Hornbee took a cup from a shelf and ladled some cider into it. He knelt down beside Matt and blew into the cup, testing to see if it was cool enough to drink.

"It's hot, lad, but it will do you good," he said, carefully offering the cup to Matt.

Matt thanked him and took a sip. "Israel . . . my friend, is he . . . is he . . . ?"

"Yes, he's gone," Mr. Hornbee said gently. "And you were close to being gone with him. I would have passed right by if a drummer hadn't stopped me and asked me to look out for you."

"Henry?" Matt croaked.

"I don't know what his name be, but he right saved your life. I was out along the Pennington Road, returning from my sister's farm, when I met up with the militia. If I hadn't known Major Horst personally, I being a neighbor of his, I would have been taken for a spy for sure. They were that jittery, you see. But after Major Horst assured them of my loyalties, I was given clearance to proceed to my farm." Mr. Hornbee reached for a small iron hook that hung beside the fireplace. He used it to lift a lid off a pot that was covered with hot coals. Matt could smell the rich aroma of a hearty stew as Mr. Hornbee ladled some into a bowl.

"Try this, son, it will give you strength," he said, handing the bowl to Matt. "Now where was I? Oh, yes, on the Pennington Road. It was as foul a night as I've ever seen and the brave lads were trudging along, when this drummer waved me over," Mr. Hornbee explained. "He told me that you and your friend were down at the fork in the road and he asked me if I could assist you. Can you remember any of last night, then?" Mr. Hornbee looked down kindly at Matt.

Matt shuddered, looking over to the fire, as the memory of the night before came rushing back. "It's like a dream," he whispered. "Like a fantastic dream. And it got so horrible, I couldn't wake up from it. I feel like I still can't," Matt moaned.

Fifteen

THERE, THERE, SON." Mr. Hornbee had taken the bowl from Matt. "You're too young to be having to make sense of this war business, though in truth even an old man such as myself can little understand it."

"But you are a patriot, right?" Matt asked.

"Nathan Hornbee, I'll not have this talk in my house, it's too dangerous," Mrs. Hornbee interrupted. Her husband sighed heavily, motioning for Matt to try the stew.

"Temperance makes a fine stew." He smiled weakly. "But a dreadful patriot, I'm afraid." Matt tasted the stew and tried to smile.

"It's not that she's a Tory, really," Mr. Hornbee whispered as his wife went back to her loom. "It's just that she's afraid. I wouldn't sign for the King's protection papers, as many of my neighbors have.

That means our farm is open game for plundering by the British regulars and the Hessians alike, especially if it be known that we were harboring a rebel." He looked down at his gnarled hands and shook his head. "I'm an old man and I've worked my whole life for this farm. I've lost most of my fencing to this war; why they even cut down two of my apple trees for firewood. My heart is with our American boys," he whispered. "But in truth, we're too old to be part of this struggle. And you see we can't offer you shelter here, for it would be too dangerous." He lifted his weary eyes to Matt.

"I understand," Matt told him, finishing up the bowl of stew. "I have to get back across the river, anyway. My sister and friends are probably worried about me."

"And what is your family's name?" Mr. Hornbee asked.

"Uh . . . Carlton," Matt mumbled. "My name is Matthew Carlton."

"So, it's Pennsylvania you come from, Matthew Carlton?" Mr. Hornbee smiled. "Forsooth, I've never seen such dress across the river," he said, nodding in the direction of Matt's sweatshirt and jeans, which were hanging on a drying rack behind him. "Tell me, what's this contraption on your breeches called?" he asked, pointing to the zipper. "And the stitching, I've never seen such fine little stitches. Was it your sister who made them for you?" Matt could see that Mrs. Hornbee had put down her shuttle and was waiting with raised eyebrows for Matt to reply.

"No, my sister didn't make them," Matt tried to explain. "My mother bought — "

"Oh, it was your mother then," Mr. Hornbee interrupted. "Such a skilled seamstress," he marveled, fingering the topstiching on Matt's jeans.

"No, you don't under — " Matt began.

"And your shoe, Matthew," Mr. Hornbee exclaimed, picking up the red sneaker. "Who made your shoe? And what animal skin is this from?" he asked, taking a bite on the rubber sole.

Matt looked into the kindly old man's eyes and wondered if he should tell him the truth. He knew his story would be difficult to believe but Mr. Hornbee seemed so willing to listen and so kind. Matt longed to tell someone all that had happened. He took a deep breath and began.

"I'm not from Pennsylvania. I'm from America, but not your America," Matt said.

"Oh, I see. You're from the territories, are you?" Mr. Hornbee asked.

"Well, yes, I guess Nebraska would be considered the territories, but . . . well, this is going to sound strange." Matt shot a look at Mrs. Hornbee, who was watching him out of the corner of her eye. "I'm from the twentieth century," he said, looking back to Mr. Hornbee. Matt paused, watching the old man's face for a sign of surprise, but Mr. Hornbee sat, blankly staring.

"My hearing's a-faulting me, lad. What is it you said?" he asked, moving closer.

"The twentieth century. I'm from another time, from twentieth-century America," Matt told him. He explained all about the club and the camp-out and the rowboat. As Mr. Hornbee sat quietly listening, Matt began to hope that he believed his story and that maybe he could even help him find his way back home.

Matt watched as the old man looked over to his wife, who now sat on the edge of her stool with her face gone completely sour. Then Mr. Hornbee looked back to Matt and softly said, "That's all very interesting, Matthew, but tell me, son, did you receive any wound to the head of late?"

Matt's face fell. "You don't believe me, do you?"

"There, there, Matthew." Mr. Hornbee reached out and patted Matt's shoulder. "Temperance, I don't think we can let this boy off on his own, he's been affected, that's plain." The old man looked over pleadingly to his wife.

"Just so," Mrs. Hornbee said, standing. "But he's more a danger to us now than ever. If he's questioned in our house, there's no relying on what he'll answer. We could lose everything, including our necks! No, he's got to get dressed and leave at once," she said emphatically. Mr. Hornbee lowered

91

his eyes. "At once, Nathan, do you hear me? At once!" she snapped, glaring at her husband as she marched out of the room.

"Ah, she's a kind woman, really. Just frightened, she is." Mr. Hornbee sighed. Matt wondered just which one of them he was trying to convince.

It wasn't long before Matt had put his clothes back on. They felt warm and toasty after hanging in front of the fire. Mr. Hornbee wouldn't let him out of the door without giving him a deerskin coat that the old man claimed he had gotten too heavy for.

"Come along then, and we'll saddle up Blackjack," Mr. Hornbee said, reaching for his hat.

"Blackjack?" Matt asked, following him outside to the barn.

"My mule," Mr. Hornbee replied. "He'll follow the trail through the woods and take you right to the river. He's smarter than any horse you've ever been on, I'll wager."

Matt watched uneasily as the long-eared, sleepy-looking Blackjack was led from the barn. Matt wanted to tell the old man that he had never been on a horse before, much less a mule. *A skateboard, Mr. Hornbee. That's the last thing I rode on,* Matt was thinking as he watched Blackjack open his mouth in a big-toothed yawn.

"You can take care of your business yonder, son," Mr. Hornbee told him, nodding toward a little shed behind the house.

"My business?" Matt asked with a blank look.

The old man shook his head and sighed heavily. "Surely that head wound has left you confused," he said, gently leading Matt to the shed. "Come along, now." And he opened the door and gave Matt a little push inside.

"Oh, that business!" Matt smiled, on discovering that the shed was an outhouse. As he sat on the crude wooden seat, Matt thought of his bathroom at home, with its fancy marble sink and cushioned toilet seat. He looked down at the hard frozen ground and thought of his bathroom's plush pink wall-to-wall carpet. He sighed, thinking of the Jacuzzi that his father had just installed.

I never thought I'd admit it, but a bathtub sure would look good about now, he thought. *And a roll of toilet paper would look even better!*

Meanwhile, Mr. Hornbee was having a conversation with Blackjack. "You're to take him to the river, then," the old man whispered to the mule. "And I trust you'll keep to the trail. The lad's a bit daft, you see, so it will be up to you, old boy, to look after him."

Matt found the two waiting out on the road in front of the house. He looked warily at the mule and took a step toward him.

"You've nothing to fear," Mr. Hornbee smiled, on seeing Matt's worried look. "You'll not find a smarter animal," he assured him as he helped Matt climb up on the mule. "Now, the first house you come to is just before the River Road. It's my cousin's farm and you can leave him there. Blackjack will know enough to wait for me, till I can come and pick him up. You'll have to manage as best you can finding passage across the river. If all goes well this morning you should be able to return as you came, though in truth it's a miracle you crossed at all with the river being as it is." The old man frowned. "I'm sorry that I can't take you as far as the river myself, but my Temperance is sick with worry about the troops being so close, and I dare not leave her again."

"Oh, that's all right," Matt said, as bravely as he could from atop the mule. The day was overcast and when Matt looked toward the woods, he could see the threatening storm clouds gathering above the tree line. Just then the door of the house opened and Temperance Hornbee came flying out. Matt felt himself stiffening, as he expected some shrill send-off from the old woman. She said nothing though, as she walked up to Blackjack and offered him a handful of crumbs. Then she brought out her other hand from behind her back and Matt could see that she was holding a pair of shoes.

"It's not the season to be without shoes," she said, quietly handing Matt a pair of wool socks and old shoes. She quickly turned and, without another word, hurried back into the house.

"Thank you," Matt mumbled, embarrassed by her sudden gesture of kindness. Mr. Hornbee came up beside him, with his eyes twinkling. "Didn't I tell you she had a soft heart," he whispered, untying

Matt's sneaker and helping him to unravel the linen rags that he had wrapped on his other foot. The shoes were a little big, but the socks were so heavy that they took up the extra space.

"They'll be fine, thanks." Matt smiled, looking down at the old buckled shoes. Then he remembered Israel's beads. "Mr. Hornbee, do you think you can do one more favor for me?" Matt asked, reaching into his sweatshirt pocket. "Oh, no!" he suddenly cried, on finding the pocket empty.

"Here now, what is it, son?" the old man asked.

"The beads! They're gone! My friend's beads, they were in my pocket in a leather bag last night. I have to get them to his sister. I promised Israel I would," Matt cried.

"Let me have a look in the house," Mr. Hornbee suggested. "They may have dropped out of your pocket when we hung up your clothes to dry." He went in the house to search for the beads, only to come out empty-handed a few minutes later.

"I'm afraid they're not there, Matthew," he said, shaking his head. "They must have fallen out of your pocket before you arrived."

Matt felt profound sadness at having to break his promise to Israel. Unable to hide his disappointment, he thanked Mr. Hornbee for looking and for all of his help and kindness.

"I only wish I could have done more." Mr. Hornbee sighed. "Don't you think too badly of us, Matthew," he said, holding Matt's sneaker to his chest.

"And God be with you." Then he gave the mule a slap on his rump and the animal headed slowly for the woods.

Matt turned around several times to wave good-bye. He was glad that Mr. Hornbee had not gone back in the house. It was the same feeling he had when he was in kindergarten and he wanted his mother to stand in front of the house waving until the school bus pulled away. Only now instead of a school bus he was riding away on a mule! He turned around for one last look at the safety of the Hornbee farm, and he could just make out the old man standing in his doorway, waving with one hand while holding the red sneaker in the other.

Matt took a deep breath as he and Blackjack entered the woods. The powerful aroma of pine was everywhere. Matt had never smelled anything so fresh and beautiful. *So this is what America was like two hundred years ago,* he thought, riding past the magnificent evergreens. He felt as if he had entered a fairyland of trees iced with frost. Everything seemed so alive and unspoiled. There weren't any highways with cars or trucks rushing by, no planes overhead, no fast food restaurants or shopping centers. It seemed so strange and different, this America, and yet when he thought about the people he had met, he realized they weren't that different from the people of his own time.

He thought of Mrs. Hornbee and how she reminded him of his Mrs. Pritchet, his second-grade teacher, so much so that Matt wondered if she wasn't Mrs. Pritchet's ancestor. And Mr. Hornbee was not unlike Matt's grandfather. Why even Henry Schudder, now that he thought about it, reminded Matt of the bus guard on his school bus.

And Israel, who was Israel like? Matt wondered. He felt the tears coming to his eyes as he thought about his friend. Israel was special, Matt decided, like no one else. He was the older brother Matt had always dreamed of having.

Riding along, thinking of Israel, Matt sadly thought about the beads and his broken promise.

He rode for a long while unable to think of anything else. Matt felt ashamed that he had let his friend down. He felt so sad and lonely that he began to talk to Blackjack. Matt told him all about Israel and all they'd been through together. He even told Blackjack about his secret wish to have an older brother, someone just like Israel. Blackjack was very quiet as Matt talked, and every now and then he would turn his head, so as not to miss any of Matt's conversation. Blackjack was a very good listener.

They were so busy with their discussion that Matt hadn't noticed how far into the woods Blackjack had taken him. Suddenly a strange noise made the mule jerk his head sharply to the left. Matt heard the noise again, only this time it seemed to be coming from the right. He felt a shiver run through him. It almost sounded like some kind of strange bird call. "Did you hear that, Blackjack?" Matt whispered, nervously. "Did that sound like a bird to you?" But Blackjack didn't answer as he carefully made his way along the trail, taking them further and further into the darkness of the lush forest.

Matt flinched at the sound of another call. "Some strange birds in these woods, huh, Blackjack?" he croaked. "Or maybe it was a rabbit. My friend Hooter had a rabbit once that got its foot caught in a lawn mower. Kind of sounded like that. But I guess you don't have any lawn mowers around here, do you?" Matt whispered.

Blackjack wasn't thinking about lawn mowers or rabbits or birds, though. Blackjack, as Mr. Hornbee had said, was one smart mule and he knew what Indians sounded like when he heard them!

Sixteen

"IT SURE IS CREEPY in here, Blackjack," Matt whispered as he and the old mule made their way further along the trail. The strange noises that they had been hearing were now followed by the rustling of leaves. He turned around slowly and was looking behind him when the mule suddenly came to an abrupt stop. Matt quickly turned in his seat to find two Indians standing on the trail before him.

They were dressed in deerskin shirts and pants. Their long black hair fell down to their shoulders. One raised a tomahawk while the other held a bow with a long arrow pointed directly at Matt's heart! They didn't appear to be much older than Matt, but this didn't lessen his terror, for though they were just children, these Indian boys displayed a fierceness and a courage that Matt had never seen in boys before. Looking into their unblinking dark eyes, he felt the commanding presence of their strength. It left him feeling weak and soft and frightened.

Matt found himself doing what he always did when he was truly terrified. He closed his eyes. He had never been able to watch a horror movie on TV all the way through without closing his eyes and asking Katie to tell him what was happening. There was no one to tell him what was happening now, so he just sat with his eyes shut tight, listening and waiting.

Suddenly he heard some leaves rustling and more footsteps. Matt tried to squeeze his eyes shut tighter. *There's more of them!* he thought frantically. *Probably a whole tribe! I'll never live to —* Before he could finish his thought he heard someone speak.

"Oh, my gosh! Doesn't that look like the Chief?" came a voice from the bushes.

Matt cracked one eye open to see the two Indians still standing before him. Then he opened the other eye to see Hooter, looking out from behind the bushes.

"Hoot!" Matt cried out loud.

But on hearing this the Indians thought he was giving some kind of war cry and they rushed the mule and pulled Matt off.

"No!" Hooter yelled, jumping out of the bushes and coming to Matt's aid. "Friend! He's friend," Hooter tried to explain.

"Hooter, I don't think I've ever been so glad to

see anybody in my whole life!" Matt exclaimed as the two boys embraced.

"You look awfully good to us, too," came another familiar voice from the bushes. Matt looked over to see Tony coming into the clearing.

"Tony!" Matt shouted as Tony joined their embrace, and the three boys jumped up and down for joy, all trying to talk at once.

"Where are Katie and Q?" Matt asked, looking back to the bushes.

"We've got some bad news, Matt," Tony began. Matt looked over to the two Indians. They had relaxed on seeing that Matt meant no harm. While they waited for the boys to talk they were busy picking berries from a bush along the trail. Matt turned back to Tony.

"Katie, is she hurt?" he cried.

"No, she's okay," Tony told him.

"Well, kind of okay," Hooter added.

"What do you mean, 'kind of okay'?" Matt asked anxiously. "Why aren't you with her across the river?"

"She's not hurt Matt, believe me. This is what happened." Tony tried to sound calm. "We never made it across the river last night. First Adam Hibbs fell on his gun. The bayonet stuck him right in the stomach. They said he had never had a bayonet on his musket before. I guess most of the men haven't and they weren't used to using them. Anyway, it was pretty bad."

"They don't have telephones to dial 911, or rescue squads to take you to the hospital when you get hurt," Hooter interrupted.

"So what happened next?" Matt asked impatiently. Tony squirmed and continued in a whisper.

"Then our boat hit this chunk of ice and started to go under," he said softly.

"Oh, no!" Matt gasped.

"It's okay, Matt, really," Hooter assured him. "We were rescued by a flat boat that was crossing with some horses. They had to let the horses off so we could all fit on, though. That was horrible, to watch those horses trying to swim, and then Adam Hibbs, well he was bleeding so much . . ." Hooter's voice trailed off and Tony continued.

"Anyway we came back to the shore with Adam Hibbs. They laid him next to a fire and told us to wait with him until they could get another boat to cross with."

Hooter's eyes suddenly filled with tears. "He was in a lot of pain, and they all thought he was hallucinating or something because he kept saying that he knew we were from another time."

"It was the same Adam Hibbs that was lost on the lake, then?" Matt asked.

"No," Hooter said. "It was his grandson. Adam explained to us that his grandfather had told him this fantastic story all about traveling through time in a rowboat. His grandfather told him to look out for the old rowboat and if there was anyone in it not to be surprised if they were dressed in strange-looking clothes. I think he was really glad to see us and know that his grandfather was telling the truth."

"He was in such pain though, that it was hard for him to talk," Tony added. "It got so that he could only whisper and so Q had to bend down to hear him. Most of the stuff about his grandfather he whispered to Q."

"But where is Q? And where is Katie?" Matt asked anxiously.

"I'm getting to that." Tony winced. "This officer told us to stay with Adam Hibbs until he came back for us. He went off looking for a boat, and then Adam, well Adam closed his eyes and he never opened them again. We sort of just sat there waiting by ourselves."

"Then Katie saw it," Hooter interrupted.

"Katie saw what?" Matt asked.

"The old rowboat, the one we came in," Tony explained. "It was tied to a boat that had just come over from the other side of the river. The soldiers must have found it in the ice jam on their way across."

"We heard some officers talking about it," Hooter told him. "They said the rowboat was too small to carry many men across, but that it should be saved in case they needed it later. They told two soldiers to drag the boat into some bushes to hide it."

"You remember how you said Q was to be our brain?" Tony interrupted. "Well, he had this idea that we should find you and then all get back in the rowboat. He was sure from what Adam Hibbs told him that it could get us back home. So it sounded like a good plan, didn't it?" He waited for Matt to agree.

"I don't know. I guess so," Matt said impatiently. "Go on. What happened next?"

"Well, I guess it wasn't such a good plan after all because things didn't work out the way we wanted." Tony hesitated.

"Will you just spit it out, Tony?" Matt pleaded.

"Okay, okay," Tony continued. "Since no one was really watching us it was easy to slip away from the shore. The soldiers were all so busy unloading the boats and forming into regiments, no one even missed us. We made our way into the woods, just above the river. I scouted ahead of everyone. . . ."

"Yeah, about three inches ahead." Hooter smirked.

"Well, ahead anyway." Tony shot Hooter a smirk back. "I didn't think we should go too far into the woods and lose sight of the soldiers," he explained to Matt. "Q's plan was to follow the soldiers from the woods and then catch up with you. But because of the storm it was too hard to see where we were going, and before too long we were lost."

"It was a nightmare, Matt, really," Hooter added. "We were all so wet and cold and there was nothing around for as far as we could see but snow and trees. We were desperate to find some shelter." Matt knew from his own experience just how desperate they must have felt.

"Katie was beginning to cry," Tony continued. "She wouldn't walk any further, so we found this big old hollow tree and put her in that. Q stayed with her, while Hooter and I scouted around for some dry wood we could use to make a fire. We hadn't gone too far when we heard them." He stopped and looked over at Hooter.

"Who?" Matt cried. "Heard who?"

"The enemy," Tony told him. "I guess it was the British, but they weren't speaking English. At least it didn't sound like English. They had these fancy blue-and-white uniforms on, and big black hats that stuck way up on their heads. It almost sounded like they were talking in German."

"Oh, my gosh," Matt mumbled. "The Hessians."

"See, Tony, I told you they weren't English," Hooter said.

"So what happened then?" Matt wanted to know.

Hooter and Tony looked down at the ground, too embarrassed to meet Matt's eyes. "They carried Katie and Q off on their shoulders," Tony told him in a whisper.

"And you didn't try to stop them?" Matt cried.

"Matt, they were huge, and they had these swords," Tony tried to explain. "We started to follow them, but it was so dark and we were so tired. We stopped to rest and I guess we were falling asleep when we were woken up by our friends over here," he said, pointing to the Indians.

"They saved our lives," Hooter added. "They really know how to live in the woods. They made a fire and gave us something to eat." Hooter's voice had suddenly lowered.

"What? What is it?" Matt looked from Hooter to Tony.

"Rabbit." Tony smiled. "The Indians caught this little rabbit and roasted it over the fire. You know how Hoot gets about little animals. I keep telling him that his Big Mac was once a little calf." Tony smiled again.

"But Matt wasn't smiling. "Did the Indians see the Hessians?" he asked.

"I don't know, they don't speak much English," Tony told him.

"But the Hessians were on foot, right?" Matt asked.

"They were pretty far into the woods to be able to travel on horses," Hooter said. "And there weren't any around that we could see."

"Okay, then we know what we have to do," Matt said authoritatively.

"We do?" Hooter and Tony replied.

"We have to find the Hessians and rescue Katie and Q," Matt told them.

"Uh, that's great, Matt, but just how are we supposed to do that?" Tony asked.

"That's a good question, Tony. Now if we only

had Q here to give us a good answer," Hooter said, walking toward the Indians, who were crouched by a bush.

"We can figure this out without Q," Matt told them. "I'm the president of the club and I'll think of something, don't worry." He turned to Blackjack, who had patiently waited on the trail for him. Coming up beside the mule, Matt whispered in his ear, "You wouldn't have any ideas, would you, Blackjack?" But Blackjack just blinked his eyes and yawned. "No, I didn't think so," Matt mumbled.

Seventeen

F KATIE WAS IN THE clutches of those "blood-thirsty" Hessians, Matt knew that he had to do everything in his power to rescue her. When Henry and Israel had first told him of the mercenaries, Matt had been terrified at the thought of having to face the "giants." Now he was so worried about Katie that he was afraid he wouldn't be able to find them.

Matt walked over to Hooter and Tony, who had joined the Indian boys. They were filling a leather bag with some bright red berries they'd picked off a bush. Hooter was about to put some in his mouth when one of the Indians grabbed his hand and knocked the berries out of it.

"Whoa!" Hooter called out. "What's the matter?"

"They must not be safe for eating, Hoot. Look," Matt said, pointing to the shorter Indian, who was holding his stomach and making a face. "He's trying to show you that the berries are poison."

"So if they don't eat them, what do they do with them?" Hooter wondered aloud.

"I don't know what they do with them," Tony said as he watched the Indians continue to fill the bag. "But I bet they could tell you where all the berries are in these woods, and which ones are poisonous and which are not. I'd give anything to know the kind of stuff they know."

"You're right, Tony, you're right," Matt mumbled. "They probably do know a lot of things about these woods and if anyone could tell us where the Hessians and Katie and Q are, I bet they could."

"Well, it's too bad you can't ask them." Tony sighed.

"Who says I can't?" Matt replied, walking up to the taller Indian boy.

"Uh, we need to find the soldiers," Matt began. "Big tall men," he said, putting his hands over his head. Then he motioned to his clothes. "They have fancy uniforms and guns." Matt picked up a stick and aimed it like a gun. "And they have my little sister," he tried to tell them, getting down on his knees and walking around with his thumb in his mouth.

The Indians stood watching him in silence and then they looked at each other and began to laugh. Hooter and Tony laughed, too, for Matt did look pretty funny.

"Cut it out, guys," Matt ordered, taking his thumb out of his mouth. Suddenly he had an idea. Everyone watched as Matt reached for some red berries and then held them next to his own brown hair. "Red berries, red hair," he said, putting his thumb back in his mouth. "Do you see, little one has red hair."

The taller Indian stopped laughing as a look of recognition came over his face. He shook his head and said something to his friend. Then they both looked back to Matt, shaking their heads and pointing down the trail.

"They've seen them! They've seen them!" Matt exclaimed, suddenly standing. "Will you show me?" he asked, pointing to them and then himself.

But a worried look came over the Indians' faces and Matt realized that they, too, were afraid of the Hessian soldiers.

"I wish we had something to offer them." Matt sighed.

"I've got two dollars," Hooter said, taking the bills out of his pocket. He offered them to the Indians, but they were not impressed.

"I didn't think they're too interested in money," Tony said. "Oh, but wait, I do have something they might like." He reached in his pocket and pulled out a pocket video game. It measured just four inches long and was made of blue and white plastic. He pressed the ON button. "Here, you can try it," Tony said, offering the game to the Indians. One of them cautiously opened his hand and accepted the gift. He looked down and was astonished to see a tiny man running back and forth on the small screen. With a frightened yelp, the Indian dropped the game, and backed away from it. Tony reached down to the ground and picked it up. With a great deal of coaxing he placed the game back in the Indian's hand.

"It's a toy," Tony tried to explain. "For fun, just for fun." He reached over and pushed the tiny buttons on the bottom panel. As the miniature man jumped up and down, the Indian boy's fingers began to tremble. He was certain that some white man's magic had been used to trap the little man inside the box. He quickly turned the game over in his hand, trying to find a way to free the miniature prisoner. When he opened the door on the back, and discovered the batteries, he smiled. The batteries were blue and red and would make good trinkets for trading. He pulled them out and handed them to his friend.

"No, you've got to leave the batteries in or the game won't work," Tony told him. The Indian turned the game over and looked at the empty screen. Thinking that the tiny man must have fallen out through the door, the Indian boys knelt down on the ground and began to search for him.

Tony knelt beside the Indians. "You have to put them back in the game," he said, reaching for the batteries. The Indians, however, decided that they liked the magic box and trinkets and didn't want to part with them. They untied pouches that were fastened to their pants and into these they dropped their newly acquired gifts, then they tied their pouches tight and resumed their search. Tony finally gave up and sat down on a log to wait, with Matt and Hooter beside him.

"That video game cost me ten weeks' allowance." Tony sighed as he watched the Indian boys continue their hunt.

"Don't worry about it," Hooter told him. "You can always buy another one, once we get home."

"You mean *if* we get home," Tony said, kicking a stone.

"Don't talk like that, Tony," Hooter implored. "We're going to get home. We are, aren't we, Matt?"

Matt looked over at Hooter and tried to smile. "Sure, Hoot," he said. "We'll get home."

"Oh, really," Tony said. "And just how do you suppose that we're going to do that?"

"Uh . . . yeah, Matt," Hooter said. "How are we going to do that?" He looked back over to Matt, who had lowered his eyes to the ground.

"I don't know just yet," Matt said softly. "I don't have all the answers, you know. . . ." His voice trailed off to a whisper.

"Well, you'd better find some answers," Tony suddenly demanded. "It was your idea that we start this club and your idea that we go on the hike. You're the one that always wants to be the leader. You led us into this mess and so now you'd better figure out

112

how you're going to lead us out of it." Tony's out-burst was followed by a long silence.

Matt knew that Tony was right. He knew that if he hadn't suggested that they go on the hike, none of them would be here now. It was his responsibility to get them home safely. But how? It seemed impossible.

Matt suddenly thought of the general and the seemingly impossible situation he had placed his troops in last night; yet Matt knew that if General Washington had not ordered that dangerous cross-ing of the Delaware, the entire war may well have been lost. He knew that the taking of Trenton seemed like an impossible task, and yet it was cru-cial to the rebel cause.

"The general had everything against him last night," Matt told the others. "His army was in rags and half frozen, the river was full of ice, even the weather was against him, and yet he kept going. He could have stayed home in a warm house in Vir-ginia, but instead he was out here last night, risking his life."

"Yeah, but his home was in Virginia, miles away, not light years," Tony added.

"Tony, what the general went through last night must have seemed just as impossible as our situ-ation seems today," Matt said. "I did get you into this, but I really thought every member of this club was ready for adventure and could handle it. You have to admit we've done pretty good so far." He

113

paused, looking from Tony to Hooter. "I know it's scary to be here, but if we . . . I mean when we get home, just think of the memories we'll have, and I'll do everything I can to get us back home, I promise," Matt said with conviction.

Tony kicked another stone. "I'll believe it when I see it," he said, keeping his eyes to the ground.

"Well, I believe in you, Chief," Hooter quickly spoke up. "I know you can get us home." Matt nodded his thanks to Hooter, but couldn't help frowning. He knew that Tony didn't think he was such a good leader and he had to admit that he was full of doubts himself. But as he sat on the log, reflecting on all that he'd been through, Matt suddenly realized that he had held up pretty well. He hadn't left Israel to die by himself, and he had found the courage to go on alone into the woods with Blackjack.

I might not have all the answers, right now, Matt was thinking. *But I have faced danger and I know that I do have courage. I just hope that I have enough.* He sat staring at the ground, lost in thought. When he finally looked up, he saw the Indians, standing before them. They had given up their search and were waiting for another offering.

One of the Indians looked down at Matt's shoes. He pointed to them and said something that Matt couldn't understand.

"I think he wants your shoes, Chief," Hooter said.

"Hey, what happened to your sneakers?" Tony asked.

"It's a long story." Matt sighed. "I guess I can get along with just socks, if it means they'll help us find Katie and Q," he said, taking off the old shoes. When he handed them over, however, he was surprised to see the Indian pull off the buckles and then throw the shoes on the ground.

"I don't get it," Hooter mumbled. "You'd think that he would want to keep the shoes. It's not like there are shoe stores all over the place."

"He doesn't need a shoe store," Tony pointed out. "Just look at what he's got on his feet." Hooter and Matt looked down at the sturdy, fur-lined moccasin boots that the Indian wore. "He probably made them himself. Can you imagine making your own sneakers?"

"I guess we may know a lot about video games, but they sure know more about survival," Matt said, putting his feet back in the old shoes. Just then the Indians began walking through some bushes off to the right of the trail. They stopped and turned around, waiting for Matt and the boys to follow. Matt stood trying to decide what to do. He hated leaving Blackjack and the security of the trail, but he knew that if there was any chance of finding Katie this was it.

He walked over to Blackjack and patted his head. "Thanks for the ride, old boy. I wish I could take you with me but it looks like we're going off the trail and you'd get all tangled up in there," Matt whispered, looking into the mule's big dark eyes. Blackjack nodded patiently.

"Go on, now. Giddyap," Matt called, giving the mule a slap on the rump. But Blackjack turned his head and looked back, waiting.

"No, I can't go with you," Matt said, coming up beside him. He nuzzled his face in the mule's soft black coat. "I always thought that it would be great to have a horse. Now I know that it would be even better to have a mule. This is good-bye, Blackjack," he whispered. The old mule blinked his eyes and looked as if he were smiling.

"Go on, then. Giddyap," Matt called, slapping his rump again. This time Blackjack moved forward and didn't stop.

"Come on, Matt, they're leaving," Tony called as he and Hooter followed the Indians into the woods. Matt hurried after them, turning around to take one last look.

The old black mule seemed dwarfed by the towering evergreens that lined the path. Their silvery branches hung low with the weight of the crystallike snow. There was a faint tinkling of icicles as the wind gently wove its way through the glittering trees. It was a picture all white and iced with silver, except for the lone traveler, whose soft black fur glistened in the morning light. Matt felt tears coming to his eyes as he stood watching the little mule making his way slowly down the path.

So many good-byes, he thought. *First Israel, and then Mr. Hornbee, and now Blackjack.* And with each good-bye came the question of who and what would he find next? Would he ever find his way to Katie? Would they ever find their way home? Matt turned and followed the Indians as they moved deeper into the forest. He felt a shiver of excitement run through him as he stepped further into the wild untamed wood.

Eighteen

ONCE OFF THE TRAIL, Matt felt as if he had entered an unending maze of trees and bushes. He, Tony, and Hooter tripped over logs and fell over one another in their struggle to keep up with the Indians. Matt marveled at the ease with which his guides moved through the difficult terrain. They never seemed to take an awkward step. Each movement was light and graceful in comparison to his own clumsy gait.

After what seemed like hours of forging through forest, the Indians stopped by a small grove of trees.

"What are they stopping for?" Tony whispered. They sat watching as one of the Indians untied the bag of berries that hung from his waist. He put the bag under his foot and stepped on it. Then he took his finger and dipped it in the bag. When he took his finger out it was bright red, and he brought the reddened finger up to his face.

"Wow! War paint!" Hooter exclaimed on seeing the bright red slashes across the Indian's cheeks. Matt sat transfixed, watching the Indian boys decorate their faces. When he was younger, Matt had used his finger paints, pretending to paint himself up like an Indian warrior. Now he could hardly believe that he was seeing the real thing!

"Do you think it's really war paint?" Tony asked.

"Sh . . . sh . . ." one of the Indians suddenly whispered. He had begun to scout ahead, and had just turned around to signal them. Matt and the others stood watching as the Indian picked up a stick and held it like a gun.

"The Hessians!" Matt whispered to Hooter and Tony. Then the Indian signaled for them to follow. Matt and the boys carefully made their way behind him, as soundlessly as they could.

The Indians stopped at a large group of bushes. Standing in the cover of the shrubbery, one of them silently pointed to the right. Matt followed his gaze to see Katie and Q sitting around a campfire that was just above a creek. Three Hessian grenadiers in blue and white uniforms were sitting beside them.

Matt sighed with relief on seeing his sister. Then he looked over to the soldiers. *So those are the bloodthirsty giants,* he thought. They did seem imposing in their fine uniforms and heavy black boots that went up past their knees. The men had strong broad faces with thick mustaches. As one of the soldiers stood up to tend the fire, Matt could see that he was no taller than most men and, if anything, a bit on the short side. Then the soldier reached for his black fur hat that was on the ground.

So, that's why they look like giants, Matt thought, on seeing the soldier put on the long cone-shaped hat. It stood almost two feet above his head! Matt looked over at the three muskets that stood leaning against a tree. Their bayonets were polished to a high gleam.

While they weren't the bloodthirsty giants he was expecting, Matt could see that these Hessians were still a formidable foe. Their uniforms and weapons were those of the professional soldier, and unlike the ragged American rebels, Matt knew that these soldiers had been highly trained for professional warfare.

The Indian boys seemed to sense this, too, and began to back away.

"No, we can't leave," Matt pleaded. "I have to rescue my sister." But the Indians shook their heads and turned around, disappearing into the woods. Matt, Tony, and Hooter stood staring after them.

"What did they put all that war paint on for, if they aren't going to stay and fight?" Hooter whispered.

"I guess it wasn't war paint," Matt muttered.

"I hate to say it," Hooter whispered. "But I think they have the right idea. We're no match for these guys. Maybe we could catch up if we hurry," he said, turning around in the direction of the Indians.

"Tony, where's your sense of loyalty?" Matt exclaimed, grabbing his sleeve. "That's Katie and Q over there. They are fellow club members, part of our tribe, don't you see? The Indians risked their lives to get us here. Now, it's up to us to save our people."

"But we don't even have any weapons to save them with," Tony moaned. "Those soldiers have guns and swords."

"We have courage and sticks. Just pick up a big stick," Matt ordered.

"A stick?" Tony whimpered. "Did he say a stick?"

"Maybe we could convince them that we're friends," Hooter suggested.

"It looks like Q is trying to do just that," Matt whispered, pointing to Q, who had just stood up. The boys watched in horror as one of the soldiers suddenly drew his sword and began to shout.

Q stood shaking his head. "I don't know what you want," he cried as another soldier reached over and began going through his pockets. The soldier said something in German and then pulled out a small object from Q's back pocket.

"What is it?" Hooter whispered. "What did he get?"

"I don't know," Matt replied. "It's too small to see, but whatever it is, it sure has them interested." The other two soldiers had gathered together to look down at the strange object in their comrade's hand. A look of confusion came over their faces as they tried to figure out just what the purpose of the object was.

"*Vas ist das*?" one of the soldiers demanded, looking back at Q.

"It's . . . it's a piece of bubble gum," Q blurted out. The soldier turned the gum over several times and then unwrapped it. He stood for a long while, squinting down at the tiny comic that was printed on the inside wrapper.

As Matt looked on from the bushes, he noticed that this Hessian soldier was a young burly man, with broad shoulders and a thick neck. He had a bushy brown mustache and ruddy red cheeks. His eyes were a clear crystal blue. The officer reminded Matt of Tommy from Custom Car Wash, which was just down the street from Matt's house. Matt wondered what this officer would look like washing a car. He imagined him with a hose in his hand, instead of a sword. He imagined that he would look just like Tommy, except for the mustache.

The officer suddenly looked up and smiled. "It must have been a good comic," Hooter whispered as they watched the smiling soldier hold the gum up before Q.

"It's for chewing," Q tried to explain. He pointed to his mouth and began to chew. The officer nodded and brought the gum to his nose. He smiled again, inhaling the sweet watermelon scent. Watermelon was Q's favorite flavor. The officer broke off half of the gum and handed it to Q, motioning for him to put it in his mouth.

"What does he think it is, poison?" Hooter whispered.

"He doesn't even speak English. He probably feels like he can't trust anyone," Matt whispered back. They watched Q take the gum and put it in his mouth. All the soldiers had fixed their gaze on Q, who was chewing as fast as he could.

"Now comes the best part," Q said, his voice quivering with fear. He closed his eyes and blew a big pink bubble. The soldiers all stood gaping at the strange sight of the American boy with a pink bubble coming out of his mouth. They all jumped when the bubble broke with a loud bang. Q motioned for the soldier with the gum to try it himself.

"Just take a few chews and then you can blow a bubble, yourself," Q said, pointing to the gum in the soldier's hand. The curious Hessian couldn't resist the opportunity. He slowly brought the gum to his mouth and licked it with his tongue.

"*Das ist gut!*" the soldier exclaimed. He chewed it several times and swallowed it.

"No," Q said, shaking his head. "You aren't supposed to swallow it. It's just for chewing and blowing bubbles." The soldier frowned and pointed to Q's pocket.

"I haven't any more," Q told him. "Honest, that was my last piece," he cried as the soldier began searching his other pockets. When he pulled out a wadded dollar bill, the soldier carefully unfolded it and stood staring at the face that was printed on the middle of the bill. A chill ran threw Matt, as he knew what was coming next.

"Rebel," the Hessian said sternly.

"I'm not a rebel." The boys could hear Q trying to explain. "That's just a dollar bill from my allowance."

"Can't they see he's not old enough to be a soldier?" Tony whispered.

"It doesn't matter," Matt told him. "When I worked on my history report, I read that there were a lot of American boys used as spies and runners for the rebels. If they think that Q is a spy there is no telling what they'll do to him. We've got to come up with a plan." As they watched from the bushes, the boys could see that the soldiers had laid down their muskets and were busy inspecting George Washington's portrait on the dollar bill.

"If that dollar bill can hold their attention long enough, we'll be able to sneak in, take their guns and ambush them," Matt said, trying to sound as confident as he could.

"We will?" Tony squeaked.

"Are you sure you don't want to give this some more thought," Hooter whispered.

"We don't have time for any more thought," Matt said, shaking his head. "This may be our only chance."

"But, we don't even know how to shoot those muskets," Tony objected.

"That's true," Matt said, "but the Hessians don't know that. All we have to do is point them in their direction and they'll probably surrender to us."

"Probably?" Tony asked, shaking his head.

"Don't worry, Tony," Hooter said, putting his arm around his little friend. "Matt knows what he's doing, don't you, Chief?"

"Uh . . . sure." Matt gulped. He tried to look as courageous as he could for the sake of Tony and Hooter, but his stomach hurt and he felt like crying. Matt thought of all the brave men he had met last night and hoped that he could show as much courage now. He took a step forward. Hooter followed, with Tony nervously clinging to his arm. Within seconds they reached the campfire. The soldiers were huddled together, inspecting the bill, as their muskets stood propped against a tree. Matt could hear Hooter's heavy breathing behind him, and he knew that one wrong move could well be their last. When they reached the tree, Matt took a deep breath and reached for a musket. Tony and Hooter did the same.

At the sound of their footsteps, the Hessians swung around and drew their swords. Katie screamed, Q yelled, and Matt did the one thing that he had so hoped he wouldn't. He closed his eyes and didn't move!

Nineteen

'VE GOT TO OPEN MY EYES, I'VE GOT TO! Matt was thinking frantically as he tried to find the courage to face the enemy. He had only been standing like that for an instant, when he heard Katie call his name. On opening his eyes, he saw one of the grenadiers about to charge Hooter with his sword.

"Hoot, look out," Matt yelled as he reached for a big stick that was on the ground. He threw it at the soldier, but missed him, hitting Hooter instead! Tony and Q knelt down beside Hooter as he lay moaning on the ground. The soldiers waved their swords and shouted until Matt and the boys put their hands over their heads.

"We give up!" Matt cried. "We give up!" The Hessians seemed to understand and accepted their surrender.

"Sorry, Hoot," Matt whispered as Hooter stood beside him, holding his hand over the cut on his head. The soldiers motioned for everyone to form a line, but Katie ran to Matt and wouldn't let go of his leg. One of the soldiers, a man with bright red hair and mustache, yelled something in German at her, but she wouldn't leave Matt's side. The soldier lifted his sword and growled. Katie began to sob, but didn't budge. The soldier took a step toward them. Suddenly one of the other soldiers reached out and grabbed his comrade's arm. He spoke in a low calm voice. The redheaded soldier lowered his sword and backed away. Katie's sobs had quieted down to a whimper.

The other Hessian came over to them and patted Katie on the head. Then he turned to Matt and asked, *"Das who?"*

"Uh, *das Kati*e. Her name is Katie," Matt said.

"Katie, ya! Das Katie!" The soldier looked down at Katie and grinned. Then he walked over to Hooter, who stood holding his head. There was a short gash on Hooter's forehead and it was bleeding down the side of his face. The soldier pulled a rag from his pocket and offered it to him.

"Das who?" He looked at Hooter.

"Hooter," Hooter replied as he put the rag to his forehead.

The soldier laughed. *"Hoot, Hoot,"* he repeated. When Hooter lifted the rag, his cut was still bleeding. He turned to the soldier. "If you don't mind," he said, "that is, if it would be okay with you, could I just put a little Band-Aid on it?"

"Where are you going to get a Band-Aid?" Q whispered.

"Right here," Hooter whispered back, slowly putting his hand in his pocket. The soldier shouted on seeing him reach into his pocket, and poked him with the musket. Hooter quickly pulled out the Band-Aid and held it up in his trembling fingers. The soldiers gathered around him as he opened the wrapper.

"It's okay," Hooter assured them. "It's just a Band-Aid." He pulled the end tabs off the Band-Aid and placed it over his cut. The soldiers took turns running their fingers over the smooth plastic surface. They shook their heads, bewildered at the strange material that stuck by itself to Hooter's forehead.

Everyone suddenly looked up at the sound of an approaching deer. It was a large buck that had come to the creek for a drink. Once it had picked up their scent, however, it bolted over some low bushes and ran off into the forest. The soldiers decided to try and follow the deer, since they hadn't eaten meat in many days. It was agreed that two of the soldiers would go after the deer, while the remaining soldier would take the children back to camp.

Matt was glad that they hadn't been left with the redheaded soldier, for he had looked mean. This soldier seemed much kinder. He had them march in a single file, though he allowed Katie to walk at Matt's side. He even let them talk amongst themselves when they stopped to rest. They knew that he couldn't understand English, and so were able to talk freely in front of him. It was a slow march through the woods, and they stopped several times to rest as the day wore on.

"At least we're all together, finally." Matt sighed when they had come to another stop.

"Yeah, great," Tony whispered. "And now we can all die together."

"I want Mommy, Mattie-o," Katie cried, on hearing this. She clutched Matt's leg.

"It's okay, Katie, no one is going to die," Matt whispered. He turned around to face Tony. "No one in this club is going to die. Do you understand? I'm going to get us out of this. I promise."

"How are you going to get us back home? Back to the twentieth century?" Tony wanted to know.

"The rowboat," Q said. "If we find the rowboat, maybe we can get back home."

"Maybe?" Matt asked, turning to Q.

"I'm afraid it's only a maybe," Q told him. "Adam Hibbs said his grandfather had traveled through many different time periods in the old rowboat before he found this one."

"Wow," Matt whispered.

"Well, I guess it seemed like such a fantastic story that no one but his grandson believed him," Q added.

"But did Adam Hibbs ever try and get back to his own time?" Matt wanted to know.

"No, he decided to stay in this one," Q replied.

"Why?" Tony asked.

"From what Adam said, the young Adam that is, his grandmother was very pretty. He said that his grandfather took one look at her and decided that the 1700s would be as good a time as any to call home."

"Oh, yuck!" Tony said, making a face.

"After he decided to stay in this time," Q continued, "he hid the boat, but someone else must have found it, because it disappeared and he never saw it again. He told his grandson the whole story, and the young Adam had been looking out for the old boat ever since he was a boy."

"But, Q, did he tell you how his grandfather knew where the boat would take him? Did he have any control over what time he could travel to?" Matt asked.

Q shook his head. "He was getting to that, but his voice got so low, I just couldn't make out the words. Something about the 'mind.' It was the last thing that he was trying to tell me before he closed his eyes and . . . well . . . you know, stopped talking," Q said, looking away.

"Oh, great!" Matt moaned. "Now we just have to find the rowboat and take our chances."

"What do you mean 'take our chances'?" Hooter wanted to know.

"He means maybe we'll get back to our time and maybe we won't," Tony told him.

"And if we don't, there's no telling where we'll end up," Q said.

"I want to go home!" Katie cried. "I want Mommy!"

"Shhh . . . Katie, don't worry," Matt said, bending down to hug her. "I'm here with you, and we'll find a way to get back home to Mom and Dad, really we will."

He looked up to see the worried faces of Tony, Hooter, and Q. "We'll do it. We will," he tried to assure them. "But first we have to get ourselves away from these Hessians and back with the American Army," he whispered.

"Where are they?" Hooter wanted to know. "All I see is trees and more trees."

"And even if we did know where the rebels were, how are we supposed to get to them? He hasn't let go of that musket since we started," Tony said, nodding to the Hessian.

As he looked over at the soldier, Matt tried to guess his age. *If you took away the mustache,* he thought to himself, *he wouldn't look much older than Israel.* Matt couldn't get the young soldier out of his mind.

"Why do you suppose the Hessians came all the way over here from Germany to fight in a war they didn't know anything about?" he whispered to Q.

"Well, King George was running out of British

troops to send over to America, so he paid the Germans to send some of their troops," Q told him.

"Do you think they're really as bloodthirsty as the rebels say?" Matt asked.

"I don't know," Q answered. "I suppose some are and some aren't. But by the looks of this one, I'd say they're a lot like any other soldier. They're just trained differently. I remember reading about it for our report. Actually many of their soldiers were young boys who lived on farms and needed the money or wanted to become somebody special."

"Like a marine?" Hooter asked.

"I guess you could say they were like marines." Q nodded.

"I wouldn't mind being a marine and protecting my country," Hooter said. "As long as I wouldn't have to hurt anybody."

"I don't think it works like that, Hoot." Matt smiled, but he knew what Hooter meant. Suddenly the soldier sighed loudly, and pulled up his pant leg, just above the boot line. He had walked through some thorny bushes and his leg was beginning to bleed. Hooter reached into his pocket and pulled out the biggest Band-Aid he had. He always carried Band-Aids, in case he met someone who needed one. And he always carried three different sizes.

"Uh . . . excuse me, sir," he said loudly. "But would you like a Band-Aid?" He waved it in the air in front of the soldier. "Band-Aid, Band-Aid," he said. He waited to see the soldier's response and, when the Hessian beckoned him forward, Hooter stood up. He went up to the soldier and opened the Band-Aid and carefully placed it over the bloodiest part of the wound. The leg was pretty badly scratched, but the Band-Aid was able to stop the severest bleeding.

The soldier stared at the Band-Aid for a long time and pulled at the edges, feeling the sticky underside. Then he looked at Hooter.

"Ban . . . Bandad. Ho . . . Hoot!" He smiled at Hooter and then tapped himself on the chest. *"Ich bin Gustav."*

"Gustav, that's great!" Hooter grinned. "Hi, Gustav, nice to meet you."

"Ya, ya, Hoot!" The soldier grinned back. Then he stood up and had them form into a line again.

"Hooter, we aren't at a tea party," Matt said sternly as they began to make their way through the woods. "We're not supposed to be making friends with them. That's the enemy." He nodded warily back at the soldier. They continued the march in silence, until the sounds of rushing water filled their ears. As they came into a clearing, they found themselves suddenly standing on the banks of the Delaware.

"It's the river!" Matt whispered. "This is probably our best chance to meet up with the army." He turned around to look at Gustav. The soldier had a confused look on his face, as if he were lost. He pointed his musket down to the shoreline and mumbled something in German.

The weary prisoners trudged on down to the shore and walked along the water's edge. They had only walked a few yards when they came upon a fat beaver building a dam. The beaver was off to the left side of the shore and was so intent on his work that he took no notice of the group. Even Gustav seemed to be interested, as they all stopped to observe the industrious animal.

Katie stood beside Matt, but her attention was diverted to a family of wild ducks that were floating on the river. She took a few steps in their direction.

As everyone was preoccupied with watching the beaver, they failed to see Katie moving closer to the river's edge. When she spotted a baby duck in the group, she stepped further out onto the ice, hoping to get a better look.

"Help," Katie cried suddenly as the thin ice cracked and her left leg disappeared into a hole.

Before Matt could move, he saw that Gustav was up and running to the edge of the ice.

"Don't move, don't move," Matt called out to Katie, who was struggling to free her leg. He and the rest of the boys had rushed over and were now gathered along the shore watching, as Gustav bravely made his way onto the thin ice. Matt knew that if the ice cracked and Gustav fell through, he would surely die. But the Hessian soldier didn't hesitate for a moment. His eyes were riveted to each step he took, knowing full well that the next step could well be his last. When he reached Katie, he pulled her leg free and quickly carried her off the ice that shuddered and cracked beneath his feet. It was the bravest thing that Matt had ever seen anyone do.

Once they had reached solid ground, Gustav put Katie down and she ran crying to Matt.

"*Katie!*" Matt scolded as he picked her up. "You manage to get yourself in more trouble than the whole club put together! You could have drowned!"

Matt looked over guiltily at the Hessian soldier. He felt bad about his earlier remark, referring to Gustav as the enemy. He knew he should thank him for saving Katie's life, but he was too embarrassed to go up to him, though Hooter was not.

"Thanks, Gustav," Hooter cried, holding his hand out to the soldier.

Gustav smiled and shook Hooter's hand.

"That was a really brave — "

But Hooter's voice was suddenly silenced by the sound of musket fire. He and the rest of the club looked on in horror as Gustav cried out in pain, for a musket ball had ripped through his back. He took a step, then fell forward, toppling to the ground, with his face in the snow.

"Cease your fire. The rest are just children," came a loud voice. Matt and the others stood staring, wide-eyed, as a group of rebel soldiers came out of the woods. A skinny-looking corporal went up to Gustav and poked him hard with his musket.

"I don't think this Hessian will be causing us much trouble now," he called back to his comrades with a grin. "You see, boys," he continued, "here is one Hessian you can trust."

Twenty

No!" HOOTER SCREAMED. "Gustav! Gustav!" he cried, sinking to the ground. The rebels stood staring with puzzled looks. They raised their muskets.

"So, we're dealing with some Tory spies, are we?" a ragged soldier said, pointing his gun at Hooter.

"No, we're patriots," Matt cried out. But the rebels looked on warily as Hooter knelt crying beside Gustav.

"If you're patriots, what are you doing with the likes of this scum?" a soldier asked, motioning to the slain Hessian.

"We were his prisoners." Matt tried to explain. "He captured us in the woods back there, and my little sister walked out onto the river and almost fell through the ice. He . . . he saved her life and we were just grateful, that's all. We're patriots, really we are."

"Patriots, grateful to the enemy? What double-talk would this be?" the corporal muttered.

"Sounds like Tory double-talk to me," another rebel replied. He began to frisk the boys, digging into their pockets, but stopped when he came to a crumpled dollar bill in Tony's pocket. He handed it to one of the other rebels, and the soldiers gathered around to inspect it.

"Look, it's got a picture of the general on it," the skinny corporal said, turning the bill over.

" 'The United States of America'," he read. "But it be a strange color paper." The private frowned. "And not like any Continental currency I've ever seen."

Matt shut his eyes tightly. What would the men do if they noticed the date on the bill?

"It could be false currency that the redcoats provide their spies, in the event they're captured," another soldier suggested.

"Yes, that's likely," the corporal replied. "We'll just leave it to the captain to decide. He should be bringing down the regiment by now."

"We're not spies, I tell you, we're not," Matt tried once more to explain.

"Save your breath," a dirty-looking soldier said, pointing his musket at Matt's heart. "It's up to the captain to decide and, if he decides that you're runners, you'll probably rot the rest of your days in jail, along with the other turncoats."

"But . . . but we're only kids. My sister is only

seven years old. There's no one to look after her," Matt said, pulling Katie to him.

"The two little ones will be given homes. Good patriot homes," the soldier told him, looking at Katie and then Tony.

It was the first time in his life that Tony was actually glad to be so small. He brought his thumb up to his mouth and began to suck on it, just in case he didn't look young enough. He took it out though on seeing Matt frown in his direction.

"Don't worry," the corporal said. "The little ones will be raised to be patriots, free patriots."

But Matt was worried. They had come so close to finding their way back home, and now they were suddenly closer to spending the rest of their lives shut up in some prison! The hardest part for Matt to swallow was that it wasn't the enemy who was responsible.

He and the rest of the club stood watching as one of the rebel soldiers roughly pulled off Gustav's tall black hat and put in on his own head. The other men laughed and hooted, as the soldier pranced around with the hat tilted on his head and a smirk on his face. Matt suddenly felt sick to his stomach. He hated to see them acting so badly, for these were his rebels. They were the special brave men that he had always dreamed about and suddenly they seemed neither special nor brave.

Matt looked away, unable to watch anymore, as the soldiers laughed and made fun of the dead man.

It was as if Gustav had never been a person. Matt turned his head, and he suddenly noticed that one of the soldiers who was watching the spectacle had a small leather pouch tied to his belt. As Matt looked on, he saw the soldier untie the little leather bag and empty it out into his hand.

"I'll wager you'd get a smile from your wife if you'd be bringing home these," the soldier said to a stout corporal standing beside him. Matt's mouth dropped open as he saw the handful of blue beads.

"Where did you get these from, Gabe?" the other corporal asked, looking over the beads.

"I found them in the snow on the march back," the soldier answered. "And for a small price the little beauties are yours."

Matt was about to call to him, when the soldier holding the beads suddenly looked up.

"Here's the regiment, now," he said, nodding toward the woods. Matt and the others turned to see a larger group of soldiers making their way to the shore. Matt didn't want to take his eyes off the beads and quickly turned back to watch the soldier drop them back into the pouch and tie it on his belt.

Soon, the shoreline began to fill up with troops. Matt knew that after their success in Trenton, the rebels must have been feeling victorious, despite the exhausted look on their faces.

If only Israel hadn't gotten sick, Matt thought. *We would have been walking out of the woods, to-*

gether, right now. His eyes filled with tears as he stood watching.

"What do we have here?" a familiar voice suddenly boomed. Matt wiped the tears from his eyes in time to see Captain McCowly standing before him.

"Runners, Captain. Look like runners to me, anyway," one of the soldiers replied. "Found them with this Hessian," he said, pointing to Gustav's body.

"Um . . ." The captain looked over the trembling members of the Adventure Club and suddenly focused on Matt.

"Captain, it's me!" Matt sputtered. "Remember I was bringing the general his cape."

A look of vague recognition came over the captain's face. He turned to spit in the snow just as General Washington walked up behind him. His spittle landed inches from the general's boot.

"Your Excellency! I beg your pardon, sir. I didn't see you approaching," the captain stammered.

"It's of little concern," the general said. He walked over to Matt. "So it was you who was responsible for returning my cloak?" he asked.

Matt was awestruck. He didn't know what to say. He didn't even know if he could get any words out.

"Uh . . . uh . . . yes, sir," he managed to croak.

"It was a bitter night," the general said solemnly, "but the morning was as sweet as any I've known." He looked out over the river, his eyelids heavy with lack of sleep. Matt knew he was talking about the victory at Trenton. Suddenly the general noticed Katie and motioned for her to come to him.

"Well, well, my little lady," the general whispered as he knelt with Katie on his knee. "You seem to have gotten your feet wet once again." Katie nodded and stuck her thumb in her mouth. "There's a little girl just about your age waiting for me back at Mount Vernon," he told her. Katie smiled on hearing this.

"And do you know," the general continued. "That little girl clucks over me just as much as Mrs. Washington. Yes, and whenever I have to be away from home, that little lady insists on my taking an extra pair of stockings." He winked at Katie as he pulled a pair of woolen socks from his overcoat pocket and gave them to her. Then he put her down and motioned for Matt to come forward. He held out his large hand for Matt to shake.

"I thank you, sir, for the return of my cloak. It was no night to be without it, and if I can ever be of service to you please call on me," the general said.

"No, sir . . . er yes, sir . . . er I mean thank you, sir," Matt stammered. Then he had an idea. "Er . . . General, sir, if it wouldn't be too much to ask, could I speak to you alone, for a minute?"

The general seemed preoccupied as he stood watching the troops file down to the shore. His eyes were red and teary and his face looked haggard with exhaustion, yet the exhilaration of victory seemed to give him renewed energy. He still had much to oversee.

"A minute is all I have time for," the general said, motioning for Matt to come closer. "Make haste, lad. What be your concern?" he asked, placing a hand on Matt's shoulder. The two of them turned away from the others.

It took all of Matt's courage to begin, but once he did he found that it was easy to talk to the great man. Matt told him all about Israel, and Abby, and the beads. When he had finished he looked up to see a grieved look on the general's face.

"This war has taken so many," the general said in a low voice. "My heart is sickened with the sight of it, and yet I find myself called upon to lead them through this misery . . ." The general's voice trailed off and there was a long silence. Matt didn't know what to say. Finally the general spoke.

"Our victory today has brought us that much closer to the peace we all long for and the freedom we seek. Your friend will not be forgotten. I will personally see that Miss Abigail Gates receives her beads, don't worry." Then he turned and walked over to his aide, who had been waiting for him. Matt watched as the aide approached the soldier with the beads. After a few words to him, the soldier handed over the pouch. Matt backed away, glaring at the other soldiers who had been ready to throw him in prison, but the soldiers were too embarrassed to meet his gaze.

Soon the shoreline was bustling with activity, as the victorious, but exhausted troops poured in,

143

ready to be ferried back across the river. The club members watched as a group of Hessian prisoners were being led to the shore. Captain McCowly came up beside them.

"The general has ordered your return passage across the river," he said. "You're to wait here until a boat is available. Now mind you, you're under my charge until you leave this shore, so don't be wandering off, now." Without another word, he turned and disappeared back into the crowd of soldiers.

"Let's find a place we can sit down," Matt said, walking over to a big log. The rest of the club members turned and followed him, all except Hooter, who had gone back to Gustav's body. Matt walked over to him and placed his hand on Hooter's shoulder.

"He was good you know, Matt." Hooter's voice had broken into a sob. "I don't care what they say, he was good."

"Yeah, Hoot, I know," Matt whispered.

"I don't understand it," Hooter said, looking up to Matt. "Who are the good guys and who are the bad guys? It's not like on TV, where you can always tell."

"No, it's not," Matt said softly. "I thought this was supposed to be one of the good wars. The rebels were supposed to be the good guys, but maybe there's no such thing as just good guys fighting bad guys. It seems like there's good and bad on both sides. And you know, the funny thing is that sometimes they're really fighting for the same things. My friend Israel, I don't think that he was all that different from Gustav, except for the uniform. Maybe if it weren't for the different uniforms, they could have been friends, instead of ending up like this." Both boys stood staring down at the fallen soldier.

Gustav was lying on his stomach, with half his face in the snow, and the other half turned toward them. The one eye that they could see was open. And as Matt knelt down beside him, and looked into that clear blue eye, he knew that he would never forget its unblinking stare, the cold, unyielding stare of death. He thought about how warm and full of life Gustav's eyes had been, just minutes earlier. And he thought of Gustav's good-natured voice laughing. *"Das Katie, ya, das Katie."*

Matt felt the tears running down his face as his trembling fingers touched the frozen snow crystals that were forming on the dead soldier's eyelashes.

"I'm sorry," he whispered. "I'm sorry that I didn't thank you for saving my sister's life."

"I hate war," Hooter cried, his husky voice choked with pain.

"Me, too, Hoot," Matt whispered, closing Gustav's eye. "Me, too."

Twenty-one

WHEN MATT AND HOOTER returned to the group, they found that Katie was missing once again.

"Katie, where are you?" Matt yelled as he frantically scanned the shoreline. Hooter, Tony, and Q joined in the hunt.

"There she is," Tony said, finally spotting her in some bushes. Katie was sitting on a log and had slipped her little hands into the huge wool socks that the general had given her. She waved a floppy sock at them and grinned.

"Don't you dare move," Matt called. "Stay right where I can see you, and don't take another step." He sat down on a big smooth rock facing her, while the rest of the boys sat down beside him. Of course Katie couldn't resist disobeying orders. She promptly sprang up and took a big step, then sat back down on the log.

"I know something that you don't, Mattie-o," she sang.

"Not now, Katie," Matt said sternly. "You sit right there, while we figure out what to do next."

"What are our choices, Mattie-o?" Tony said in a defeated tone. "I don't see how we're ever going to get back home."

"I know something that . . ." Katie taunted.

"Katie, will you just sit down and keep quiet, so we can think?" Matt snapped. He stood up and looked out over the ice-choked river.

"Good old Rumson." Hooter sighed. "I never thought I'd miss it so much. I didn't even miss it that much when I went all the way to California to visit my grandmother."

"But, Hooter, we're not just miles away," Tony said. "We're light years away!" He bit down on his lip, trying not to cry. "I wonder if we'll ever get back," he whispered.

They were all suddenly quiet as they sat attempting to dispel their fears. Matt was trying hard not to give in to the anxiety that was overtaking him. Katie, meanwhile, was busy taking the socks off of her hands. She bent down and untied her sneakers.

"Katie, what are you doing now?" Matt asked as he watched her pull off the sneakers.

"I'm going to put these socks on my feet," she told him.

"Katie, are you crazy?" Q cried suddenly, when he saw what she was doing.

"No," Katie answered.

"His socks! Don't you realize that those are

George Washington's socks? You can't put them on your feet!" Q was horrified.

"But my feet are cold," Katie told him, slipping her little foot into one of the large socks. "And he gave them to me. Besides, my jeans are all wet and this sock is so big it goes all the way up my leg." She grinned.

"You can have my socks, we'll trade," Q offered.

"Oh, no," Katie said. "He gave them to me and I don't have to trade if I don't want to."

"What a waste." Q sighed, looking over to Matt, "George Washington's socks wasted on a girl!"

"Don't take it so hard, Q," Matt tried to console him.

"You can always try dumping yourself in the river," Tony told him. "The general might be out of socks but who knows. Maybe he would give you his underwear." Everyone laughed but Q.

"If I was lucky enough to end up with George Washington's underwear you can bet I wouldn't wear them, either," Q told him.

"What would you do with them?" Hooter wanted to know.

"I'd frame them," Q said solemnly.

"Are we going to stand around all day talking about George Washinton's underwear, or are we going to try and find the boat?" Matt asked impatiently. Everyone grew quiet as they looked back out at the swollen river.

"I know something that you don't," Katie called again.

"All right, Katie," Matt snapped. "What do you know?"

"I'm not telling, now." Katie sulked. She always did this when Matt was impatient with her.

"Oh, cut it out, Katie." Matt sighed, looking toward the river, searching for the boat.

"That river is so big," Tony moaned, "there's no telling where it may have ended up."

"Over here," Katie said softly as the boys continued to ignore her.

"Maybe we could ask some of the soldiers who are steering the boats, if they've seen it," Q suggested.

"But you can ask me," Katie said. "I've seen it." Everyone stopped talking and looked at her.

"You've seen what?" Matt asked.

"The rowboat." Katie smiled. "I've seen the rowboat.

"Where?" Matt demanded.

"Right there," Katie said, pointing to the bushes behind her. Matt and the others bolted from the rock they were sitting on and dove into the bushes. There they found the old rowboat, hidden in the weeds.

"It's here!" Hooter yelled. "It's really here!"

"Katie, what would we do without you?" Matt cried as he lifted her in his arms and swung her around.

"Does this mean that I'm a club person, now?" Katie asked, blushing with pleasure.

"A club member," Matt corrected her. "Katie, you are definitely a club member. We're going to make you associate vice president." He grinned.

"Look at this!" cried Q, who was standing alongside the boat. Matt and the others huddled beside Q as he pointed to a puddle of water that had formed on the floor of the boat. In the reflection of the water they could read backwards the chipped letters, EMIT LEVART, that were carved on the inside of the craft.

"Time travel." Matt read the letters aloud. " 'Emit Levart' spelled backwards is *time travel*!"

Everyone began talking and laughing at once; everyone except Q, who had suddenly stepped back from the boat. He stood nervously adjusting his glasses.

"There's something wrong with the boat," he said as loud as he could.

Everyone suddenly grew quiet.

"Don't you remember how we all fell under its spell as soon as we saw it? How it sort of pulled us in?"

"Q's right," Hooter said. "Why don't we feel as if we're under its power right now?" Feelings of panic began to overcome them.

"Do you think that maybe the power has all worn off?" Tony asked nervously.

"There's got to be a way to activate this thing," Q said.

150

"I can't believe it." Hooter sighed. "I can't believe that we're stuck here in the eighteenth century!"

"I'm not sticking anywhere," Katie said, and without another word she climbed into the boat.

"I'm ready to leave," she announced. Everyone watched as she settled herself down between the two seats and waited with her thumb in her mouth.

"Oh, no," Tony moaned. "It's starting to snow again." Matt and the boys stood shivering and wondering what to do.

Katie took her thumb out of her mouth. "I want to go home," she complained. "It's too cold. I want to be where it's warm." And with those words the old rowboat suddenly began to tremble.

"What's happening?" Tony squeaked.

"Quick, quick," Q called. "Everyone climb in!" Tony, Hooter, and Matt followed Q, falling over one another, as they scrambled into the boat. Matt sat down on a seat next to Hooter as the old boat began to rattle and shake, and then spin around among the weeds and the bushes.

"Where are we going?" Matt called above the loud rush of air that had encircled them.

"I don't know," Q yelled back. "But I wouldn't be surprised if it was some place warm!" And then they were gone! Vanished boat and all!

"General, General!" cried Captain McCowly as he went wildly running down the shore. General

Washington was standing next to a boat, about to depart.

"Yes, Captain, what is it?" the General asked.

"The children, General, it's the children," Captain McCowly exclaimed. "They've disappeared into thin air. I saw them myself. They were in a boat on the beach and suddenly they started to spin around and then they vanished! As Jehovah is my witness." The captain wheezed.

General Washington frowned, on surveying the captain's unruly appearance and smelling his harsh whiskey breath.

"It's not time for celebrating, yet, Captain," he said sternly.

"No, General, you don't understand! I really saw . . ." But the captain was guided away from his commander by several of the general's aides. George Washington shook his head. The victory at Trenton had been long in coming and the general knew his men deserved to celebrate, but he hated to see his officers acting so badly. He wished they would behave in a more professional manner. They should be setting examples for the other men, and drink had no place in the military as far as the general was concerned.

General Washington turned and was about to step into the boat when he tripped and fell.

"Sir, are you hurt?" an officer inquired, helping his superior to his feet.

"No, no, I'm fine, except for the soaking," the

general said on standing. The water had gotten into his boots and he could suddenly feel the wet socks sticking to his feet. He automatically reached into his overcoat pocket for his extra pair of socks. Then he smiled on remembering the little feet that were in them now. *I hope she's warm enough,* the general thought, stepping into the boat.

He needn't have worried. She was! As the members of the Adventure Club found themselves spinning through space in a cloak of darkness, they could feel the temperature rising. When the boat finally settled and the mist lifted, Matt opened his eyes, but there was not enough light to see.

"Katie?" Matt called in the darkness.

"Mattie-o?" Katie called back.

"Are you okay?" Matt asked, reaching for her.

"I'm okay," Katie answered.

"Hooter?" he called. "Are you okay?"

"Yeah, Mattie-o, I'm okay," Hooter whispered.

"Tony? How about you, still with us?" Matt called.

"Yeah, Matt, I'm here, wherever here is," Tony called back.

"Q, are you all right?" Matt asked.

"I'm okay, Matt," Q replied.

An eerie silence followed.

"Matt?" Katie called. "Do you think we're home?"

"I don't know Katie," Matt whispered. "But I know we're not on the Delaware River anymore," he said, dipping his hand in the warm still water.

Twenty-two

IF ONLY WE COULD figure out the magic of the boat," Tony whispered as they sat floating in the darkness.

"Adam Hibbs had tried to tell me about it before he died," Q spoke up. "He said something about the mind. Maybe what he was trying to tell me was that our thoughts have something to do with the power of the boat."

"You know, we were all talking and thinking about the Revolutionary War when we first saw the boat," Tony added.

"That's right, we were," Matt agreed. "And Katie was thinking about home when she got back in the boat to leave."

"We may never figure it all out, but I think we've unraveled an important thread," Q remarked, trying to sound like his hero Sherlock Holmes.

"All I know is it sure feels good to be warm again."

Matt sighed, dipping his hand into the warm lake water. "I'd almost swear we were back on Levy Lake."

"This may be the right lake, but is it the right year?" Tony wondered as he squinted in the darkness. Matt's hand skimmed along the water's surface, when suddenly he felt something float over his fingers. He jerked his hand away from it, thinking that it might be a fish. When he was finally able to make it out in the misty darkness, he realized that what was floating in the water was a piece of paper. Quickly, he bent over the side of the boat and scooped it up onto the floor of the boat.

"What is it, Matt?" Hooter asked, leaning over to see what it was. All the other members of the club did the same.

"I don't know," Matt whispered.

"Let's just hope that it's not a piece of the Continental currency," Q said. "That would mean that we're still stuck in the eighteenth century."

"Maybe it's some kind of secret message that we were meant to find," Tony suggested.

"Like a map for time travel," Hooter added. As everyone sat huddled together, trying to see the paper, the first streaks of early morning light peeked over the horizon.

"Hooter?" Matt called with a grin. "Do you think that they had potato chip bags in the eighteenth century?" Everyone laughed with relief as Matt held up the soggy potato chip bag.

As the mist slowly lifted, and the golden sun rose in the east, everyone looked out across the lake to find Tony's house nestled safely in the trees, just the way it was before they left.

"We're back! We're back!" Matt cried as everyone joined in the merry chorus of laughter and cheers.

"Look, our tent is still up!" Hooter exclaimed.

"From the looks of the light, I'd say it's early morning," Q said, adjusting the glasses on his nose.

"I wonder if my parents went off the deep end, worrying about us," Tony added. "I'm surprised they aren't out here with divers and helicopters, looking for our bodies."

"From all that I've read about time travel in my science fiction books," Q said, "it appears that a person traveling through time can experience days, weeks, and even years, and then return home to find that he's only been gone a few hours."

"That's great," Matt decided. "Maybe no one knows about our trip. Can you imagine what our parents would do to us if they ever found out where we were?"

"What about Katie?" Hooter whispered. Katie stared up at Matt.

Matt looked down at his little sister. "You know, Katie, you got yourself into some big trouble on this trip," he said sternly. "And if Mom and Dad were to find out about it, they would never let you hang out with the club again. But I don't see any reason why they have to find out, do you?"

Katie's red curls shook as she slowly turned her head from side to side. "You won't tell, will you, Matt?" she asked in a little voice.

"No, Katie, I won't tell," Matt smiled. "And Q and Tony and Hooter won't tell either, will you?" Matt asked.

"No," they all said at once.

"And you know, Katie," Matt continued, "even though you got into a bunch of trouble, you weren't as big a pain as I thought you'd be." Katie grinned as her brother reached over and gave one of her curls a gentle yank.

"Matt's right," Tony said. "We've all got to keep this a secret. I could just see my father's face, if I told him that I spent the night with George Washington's troops! He'd probably make me go to therapy or something."

"Then it's settled." Matt grinned. "We're all sworn to secrecy. We can hide the boat in some bushes, and no one will have to know about it."

"You better not go home wearing those," Q said, pointing down to the old shoes that Mr. Hornbee had given to Matt.

Matt nodded. "I almost forgot about them. My dad is going to have a fit when he finds out that I lost my new sneakers."

"Just don't try and explain how you lost them." Tony laughed. "Why don't you just throw those shoes in the lake," he suggested.

Matt looked down at the old worn shoes, and

157

smiled on remembering Mrs. Hornbee's awkward last-minute display of kindness.

"No, I don't think I'll ever throw them away," he said, pulling the old shoes off. "We can hide them with the boat. And Katie you better take off those socks. We'll keep them with the shoes."

"I don't want to." Katie frowned.

"You have to," Matt said firmly. "We'll all get into major trouble if you don't."

Katie reluctantly took off the socks and handed them to Matt, who sat waiting with his hand out. He folded the socks up and placed them inside one of the old shoes that were on the floor of the boat.

"Land ho!" Hooter cried as the boat slowly drifted to shore.

"Boy, it sure is good to be back home in the twentieth century." Matt sighed, looking over to a row of brown and green condominiums that stood between the trees. Suddenly he found himself remembering his ride through the woods on Blackjack. He remembered just how beautiful the woods were and how unspoiled the landscape was. "I'll miss the eighteenth century in a way," he whispered, standing up.

"I know what you mean," Tony agreed, standing next to him. "But if I had to be anywhere, this is right where I'd want to be." Everyone climbed out of the rowboat, everyone except Q. He was still standing in the boat, looking down at the big gray socks that Matt had tucked into the old shoes.

"Q," Matt called from the shore, "what's wrong?"

"They're his socks," Q replied. "Don't you think that it's kind of criminal to leave his socks out here?" he asked, with a pained look on his face.

"We can't take them with us," Matt told him. "Can you imagine trying to explain them to my mother?"

"But they were once on the feet of the father of our country. They should be treated with respect," Q pleaded.

"And just who was it that you had in mind to show them all this respect?" Matt smiled.

"Me! Me!" Q cried. "I could show them the utmost respect by keeping them in my own private museum, in my bedroom."

"Wouldn't your mother want to know where they came from?" Tony asked.

"No, she's given up trying to figure out where I get all my stuff from. My bone specimens and white mice scare my mom so much that she won't come in my room at all anymore, except to change the sheets on my bed. No one will ever suspect anything, I promise," he pleaded.

"It's not up to me," Matt told him, looking over to his little sister. "Katie, Q wants to know if you'll let him have George Washington's socks. You can't wear them home, so you might as well let him have them," Matt told her. Katie took a long look at the socks in Q's hand, and then she looked up into his eyes.

"I'll trade them," she said, giving one of her curls a twist.

"Sure," Q squeaked with delight. "Anything, anything you want."

"You can have the socks if you buy me my own bag of marshmallows," Katie demanded.

"You want to trade George Washington's socks for a bag of marshmallows?" Q asked, his mouth dropping open in disbelief. Katie nodded, her red curls bouncing on her head in the early morning light.

Everyone helped to drag the old rowboat across the shore and up into the woods. They found some dense bushes that made a perfect cover. When Matt was sure that the boat was safely hidden, he ordered the hike back to Tony's backyard.

"What's the first thing you're going to do when you get back to your house?" Tony asked Hooter, who was walking in front of him.

"I'm going to knock on the door and ask my parents to empty the refrigerator," Hooter told him. "I'd do it myself, but I want to save all my energy for eating." Hooter laughed. "I'll just have them shovel all the food out."

"The first thing that I'm going to do," Tony said dreamily, "is to go up to my bathroom and soak in a nice hot tub, and when I get out I'll have big soft towels and clean clothes."

"The first thing that I'm going to do when I get home is to frame George Washington's socks," Q said happily. "I'll hang them in a place of reverence over my antique snakeskin collection."

"What about you, Matt. What's the first thing that you're going to do when you get home?" Hooter wanted to know.

"The first thing that I'm going to do is to read a book," Matt said with a smile.

"Read a book?" Hooter frowned.

"Which book?" Tony asked suspiciously.

"Adventures in History." Matt grinned. This was followed by a chorus of groans from Tony, Hooter, and Q.

"Oh, don't worry," Matt told his fellow club members. "If I find anything interesting in it, I'll invite all of you for the next trip."

"Matt, you aren't serious?" Tony asked. "You can't mean that you'd really want to do this again."

"Not right away." Matt shook his head. "But some day." Everyone groaned at this suggestion. "But you have to admit," Matt whispered, "that it was an *incredible* adventure. I know I'll never forget it. I'll never forget the general's voice or Israel's face, or Mr. Hornbee or Blackjack."

"Or Gustav," Hooter added, the smile suddenly leaving his face.

"Or the Indians," Tony whispered.

"Or the baby ducks and the beaver," Katie piped in.

"Or George Washington's socks." Q sighed, holding the thick gray socks to his heart.

Twenty-three

"HOME SWEET HOME," were the only words on Matt's mind as he walked into his bedroom. He felt the warm lush carpet between his toes, and smiled at the sight of his big comfortable bed. He reached in his backpack, pulling out the thick green book, *Adventures in History*.

As Matt began to turn the pages, he found himself distracted. His eyes began drifting around the room, finally coming to rest on the silent air conditioner that sat in one of his windows. He walked over to the air conditioner and turned it on full blast. Its soft hum was music to his ears. And what about music? Matt grinned and placed a tape in his tape deck and turned up the volume.

Everything sounded and felt so good. Suddenly he remembered his reading lamp. He reached over to the wall and flipped the lamp's switch. When the light came on, Matt whooped with joy. He felt a thrill of excitement as he turned on his clock radio. He even set the alarm to go off.

"And TV!" Matt cried, racing over to his television set. "I'm going to watch TV!" By the time Mrs. Carlton appeared in the doorway, Matt was sitting on his bed reading, after turning on every electrical appliance in his room.

"What on earth is going on in here?" his mother called over the din. Matt looked up from his book and grinned.

"I was just checking to make sure that everything still works," he told her.

Mrs. Carlton shook her head. "Come and get yourself some breakfast," she told Matt. "And for heaven's sake take a bath and change your clothes."

As she walked away Matt could hear her mumble under her breath, "The way that boy looks after a simple backyard camping trip. You'd think he was just through a war!"

That night at the supper table, Matt took a seat across from Katie. Before he could stop her, Katie reached for the sugar bowl and opened the lid. The corner of her lips turned up, as a smile slowly spread across her face. She dipped two of her little fingers into the bowl, touching the sugary green peas that were still there.

"Katie, stop that right now. Put the sugar bowl down and finish your supper," Mrs. Carlton said on her way to the table. Matt watched as Katie made a face and reluctantly put the lid back on the sugar bowl.

Mr. Carlton was anxious to hear all about the camp-out. "So how was your adventure?" he asked. "Anything exciting to report?" Matt shot Katie a look as she was about to reply.

"We have to keep the club meetings a secret," Matt answered, before Katie could say anything.

"Well, they must have had some excitement," Mrs. Carlton said, shaking her head. "Their clothes were in shreds! Where were Tony's parents? Weren't there any grown-ups looking after you?"

"Just the general," Katie said truthfully.

"The general?" Mr. Carlton looked suspicious. Matt groaned and closed his eyes.

"General George Washington." Katie grinned. "He even gave me his socks." Mr. and Mrs. Carlton looked over to Matt, waiting for an explanation.

I should have known that she wouldn't be able to keep a secret, Matt thought as he sat squirming in his chair. *Now I'll have to tell them everything.*

"The truth is," he began. "We were sitting around the campfire reading this book about George Washington and the Revolutionary War and — "

"I remember doing the same kind of thing when I was a boy," Mr. Carlton interrupted. He sat back in his chair and smiled. "We would pretend that we were actually living in different times, as if we were really there. It's a great way to use your imagination.

So what are you planning for the club's next adventure?" he asked.

"Well, I'm not sure," Matt stammered. "I've got some reading to do, first."

"So you ended up with George Washington's socks, did you?" Mr. Carlton smiled over at Katie. "Weren't they a little big for you?"

"They were real big," Katie told him. "So I traded them for some marshmallows."

"Well, that was a good trade. I probably would have done the same thing." Mr. Carlton looked over to Matt and winked.

"And guess what, Dad?" Katie cried. "I'm a club member now, too, because I found the boat."

"Boat?" Mrs. Carlton's eyebrows shot up. "Oh, Matt, you didn't go anywhere near the lake, did you? You do realize how dangerous it is to play there without supervision?" She turned to her husband. "John, I told you they were too young for a camp-out."

"And one of the soldiers," Katie continued, "the nice one, who saved me from the freezing ice hole, he got killed. But George Washington, he didn't get killed."

"What a wonderful imagination the child has." Mr. Carlton beamed at Katie. "Franny, you worry too much. They were just pretending, like all kids do."

"Well, maybe you're right." Mrs. Carlton sighed. She looked at Matt and smiled. "So which one of

165

you was pretending to be George Washington?" she asked.

"Uh, well," Matt hesitated.

"Honey, I don't think Matt wants to divulge any more information." Mr. Carlton turned to Matt and whispered, "Private club business, right, son?"

"Something like that," Matt replied.

"Don't worry, your secret is safe with me, man-to-man." Mr. Carlton nodded. "You did a fine job of looking out for your sister on this camp-out and I want you to know that I'm proud of you for including her. It shows that you're becoming a mature, responsible person."

"Uh, gee . . . thanks, Dad," Matt mumbled.

"Don't mention it." Mr. Carlton smiled. "Pass me the sugar, will you, son?"

About the Author

ELVIRA WOODRUFF was born in New Jersey, where most of the Revolution was fought. She has always loved history, and once, while tubing down the Delaware River, she began thinking about what it might have been like on Christmas Eve of 1776. Being a pacifist, she wrote *George Washington's Socks* for her son Noah, who is very fond of G.I. Joe. While writing, she herself discovered the horrors of war, but also came to understand the strength and courage of those who fought. Besides spending her time writing, Elvira Woodruff visits schools and gives presentations on the Revolutionary War and on writing historical fiction.

Formerly a children's librarian and a professional storyteller, Ms. Woodruff lives in Martin's Creek, Pennsylvania.